Bleeding Heart

Bleeding Heart

Amber Stokes

~Seasons of a Story~

Cover design: Lena Goldfinch *at Stone Lily Book Designs*
Cover images: Nikki Bidgood *(model photo)*, Mtilghma *(California landscape)*, Dale *(bleeding heart photo)*

ISBN: 061586533X
ISBN-13: 978-0615865331

Praise for *Bleeding Heart*

"From first word to last, the characters, the story,
the premise of Amber Stokes's debut novel captivated and
intrigued me. This was no simple romance. BLEEDING HEART
speaks to anyone who has ever loved and lost."

~ ELIZABETH LUDWIG, Author of NO SAFE HARBOR

"A tender, heartfelt story with a maturity and emotional
intensity well beyond that of a debut novel, sure to please
readers and reviewers alike!"

~ LAURA FRANTZ, Author of LOVE'S RECKONING

Dedication

For my Heavenly Father.
Thank you for showing me what love is.

And for my daddy.
Thank you for challenging and encouraging me.

Lamentations 3:41

*"Let us lift up our heart with our hands
unto God in the heavens."*

Prologue

BREAKING SOMEONE'S HEART *should be considered a crime.* That would make Elizabeth Lawson an outlaw and Joe Clifton the victim. And that wasn't a far stretch in Joe's mind. She had rounded up his heart, branded her name across it when it should never have belonged to her, and then left him high and dry. Still, he was getting sick of hanging around the scene of the crime. He just didn't know where else to go.

Lake Tahoe had once been his favorite get-away destination, a place where he could go to just sit back and enjoy the view of water as clear as a shined-up mirror. Now those crystal depths and the unmoving boulders along the water's edge taunted him, bringing back memories of a happy proposal and another less-than-happy scene where his heart was handed back to him on a silver platter – bruised, broken, and bleeding.

He didn't want to make any more memories like that. So he made a promise to himself: He would never let anyone break his heart again.

Part I:

At My Cry

"I called upon thy name, O Lord, out of the low dungeon.
Thou hast heard my voice:
hide not thine ear at my breathing, at my cry."

Lamentations 3:55-56

Chapter 1

Virginia City, Nevada
Summer 1886

THERE WAS NO WAY on God's brown desert dirt that Sally Clay was going to marry Rufus O'Daniel.

As she hurried through town to the train station, Sally thought about how she was now in the same predicament she had been in three years ago, back when her whole world had broken into pieces as numerous as the sagebrush bushes on the hillsides. It didn't matter that Rufus was one of the wealthiest men in the whole state of Nevada – a silver baron who knew when to stop mining while others squandered their wealth away trying to make the earth give up more riches than it contained. She was through with men's tricks. This time, she was going to be the one to leave.

As much as she hated Jacob Lawson for selling his business and leaving her jobless, she recognized a glimpse of freedom when she saw it – and perhaps a foretaste of sweet, sweet revenge. The details were still undetermined, but the man had it coming to him – and soon.

Over two weeks had passed since she had been booted from her room on D Street, in "Sporting Row." She had spent most of her money, as well as some feminine persuasion toward the right man, on staying at the hotel for that time. The quiet and the independence were far more of a luxury than the fancy furnishings and the modern conveniences. But Rufus wasn't taking "no" the way she intended him to, and the desire to bolt had been building up inside of her for a long time. Now she was finally going to give in to the urge.

Spotting a familiar face in the line at the station's ticket counter, she rushed to his side. "Joe?" She touched his arm and put on her best desperate look. It wasn't too much of a challenge at this moment.

Disgust followed on the heels of recognition in his dirt-brown eyes as he looked down on her. "Whaddya want, Sally?"

She countered his question with one of her own, leaning in ever so slightly as she had been taught. "Where ya headed?"

"I don't see how that's any of yer business."

Peering around his tall frame, she saw another familiar face. For the first time since the day she found herself begging Jacob for a job, shame burned through her. It was a rare day when she blushed with embarrassment.

The red-headed, rail-thin Cornish miner – with the strange accent that alternated between lilting Irish and the familiar choppiness of the American West – didn't say a word, but she saw suppressed anger, and perhaps a hint of pity, glaring back at her. She nodded in acknowledgement, and turned her pleading gaze back to Joe.

"I know you don't owe me any favors, but you and Jacob were friends for a long time. And with Jacob leavin' and all… Well, I'm out of a job." She swallowed, longing for some water and a moment to plan the rest of her speech.

"So?"

She flinched. It shouldn't cut her anymore, these rejections. But they did. Tears welled up in her eyes – real ones, if anyone here at the train station could believe that.

"Please – I'm bein' pursued by a cruel man, and I need some help getting out of this two-bit town. Just a little bit of money and some company for as far as yer headed."

She knew the word "company" was a mistake as soon as it slipped past her lips. Joe's eyes turned rock-hard, and he shook his head vehemently.

Grasping his arm tighter, she let the tears flow down her cheeks, not caring at the scene she was making. It hadn't taken long to get over the desire to please society. They had rejected her, and so she rejected them by refusing to follow their unspoken rules.

"I don't mean it that way, Joe. Please! I won't be any trouble."

Then he had the nerve to laugh.

Pushing him away, she spun on her heel and marched out of the station. She still had some pride.

As she forced her way through the crowd and out the door, her heart sank. Rufus O'Daniel stood across the street, staring right at her with eyes that promised retribution and enslavement – a frightening look that had haunted her dreams for far too long.

Joe clenched his hands in frustration as he watched Sally storm out of the station to rain her tears on some other poor sap.

"Of all the nerve! That woman thinks she can just waltz right in here and make demands as if she means somethin' to me." He outwardly fumed, but somewhere buried deep in his soul was a connection he hadn't expected. Jacob's girls were hardly Joe's friends, but the fear he had seen in Sally's eyes surprised him. He was acquainted with her well enough to know that she was a strong woman who always seemed to get what she wanted – including the man who stole Elizabeth, or so Joe had heard. Fury slithered through him at the thought that Elizabeth still chose David over him, despite the situation with Sally.

"That gal sure does 'ave nerve, an' no mistakin' that." Myghal stood next to Joe with his arms crossed over his thin chest. Yet there was something in his expression that spoke of uncertainty.

"But...?"

Myghal looked askance at him. After a moment, he admitted, "There's somethin' botherin' me 'bout the whole thing." His lips quirked as he added, "I've always been a bit soft toward a damsel in distress."

"I think yer just soft in general, Mih-gall." Genuine gratitude edged out his anger, coupled with a smile at the sound of the butchered, "Americanized" version of Myghal's name that everyone used. "If you hadn't told me about this opportunity in California, I think I might've gone mad with restlessness. I need to get out of here."

His last statement brought Sally's big, blue, tear-filled eyes to mind. She had said the same thing, talking about her need to leave Virginia City. If there was one thing he could understand, it was the powerful, aching need to escape the past. Perhaps he should lend Sally a hand, help her get a fresh start.

"I don't owe her anythin'."

"No one said ya did," Myghal replied gently. "'Course, I don't owe you nothin', either, an' that's a fact."

Joe smirked and ran his thumb and forefinger over his moustache. "No, I don't suppose you do." If he was honest with himself, he was still skeptical of Myghal's kindness, knowing how close Myghal had been to David. But whatever the man's motives, he held out hope in all its shining glory, and Joe lacked the heart to resist. "Fine, I'll go see if I can find her. You stay here an' buy three tickets to Reno, and then on to San Francisco."

"Yessir." Myghal gave a mock salute, but his grin told Joe

who was really getting his way.

With a sigh, Joe stepped through the crowd and walked out the door, practically plowing over Sally, who stood frozen outside the building. He gripped her arms to keep her from falling face-first into the dusty road.

"Sorry 'bout that." When she failed to respond, not even grumbling about his clumsiness, he asked, "Is everythin' all right?"

She shivered, causing Joe to involuntarily rub her arms in a comforting gesture. "What's wrong?"

Following her gaze, he saw a man wearing a suit and top hat, apparently not letting the first of the early summer heat get the best of him, staring almost menacingly in their direction.

"Is that Mr. O'Daniel?" Joe doubted the man knew him, but he certainly knew of the man – as did everyone else in Virginia City. He was the epitome of what all the miners strived to be – rich.

Finally, Sally replied, "Yes." With a shake of her head and a toss of her bright blond hair, she tore out of his grasp and took off running uphill in the opposite direction of Mr. O'Daniel. Joe's surprise gave her a head start, but after a moment he sprinted after her.

"Sally! Wait!"

As he gained on her, he realized she was heading for D Street. Before she could find shelter in any of the shabby buildings, he reached out and grabbed her arm, yanking her to a stop. She screeched and slapped at his hand.

"You let me go this instant, Joe. I don't want to hear 'bout yer high and mighty ways and how a gal like me ain't fit company for an upstanding gentleman like you." Placing her free hand on her ample hip, she added, "It took a lot for me to beg like that, and well you know it. I don't need you shovin' my past in my face."

Taking a deep breath and gripping her arm just a bit tighter, he replied, "Confound it, woman. I only came out to concede defeat. You can come with us to California."

Her eyes widened and her arm went slack. "I-I can?"

"Yes, ma'am. We're headed to Eureka on the coast, so we'll take you that far, if you have a mind to head north."

She nodded and ducked her head.

"Well, come on then."

He let go and offered her his arm, like she was a real lady instead of a soiled dove. She didn't hesitate to tuck her hand close to his side. Their gazes met for a moment, and for the first time since he had known Sally, she looked meek and thankful. He wasn't fooled by her act, but it still felt good to do the right thing – and to get her away from that O'Daniel fellow who had eyed Sally like a shiny, red apple that was his for the taking.

Rufus O'Daniel was never denied anything until the day Sally Clay refused his marriage proposal. She had known the chunk of pride he was forced to swallow when he bent down on one knee and asked her. And she still threw his proposal back into his face. The ungrateful, pathetic wench.

His wealth came from silver, but it was Sally's gold hair catching the light as she boarded the train that made him hunger for things silver couldn't buy. He watched her smile at Joe Clifton, brother of Seth Clifton who owned a ranch in a nearby canyon, before disappearing from his view. Obviously, he was not a wealthy man, but still a threat. It was just like Sally to wile her way into Joe's good graces and skip town as if Rufus O'Daniel, the silver baron, was a scorned lover to be left in the dust.

Spotting a couple of young miners about to pass by him, their torn clothes covered in dirt, he roused from his bitter thoughts. He clamped a hand on one of the men's shoulders, effectively stopping them both in their tracks, relishing the wariness in their eyes and the one man's fisted hand. They *should* be cautious.

Resisting the urge to wipe his hand with the handkerchief in his coat pocket, he got right to the point. "You men know Joe Clifton?"

"Yessir," one answered, scratching at his disgusting excuse of a beard as he tilted his head in question. "What 'bout him?"

"He's about to leave on that train heading to Reno. If you men are interested in a job, I will pay you handsomely for your time."

Greed sparked in their eyes, and he knew they would listen well. He gestured to a nearby alley and waited for them to precede him into the gap between two ramshackle houses before he followed, effectively closing them in.

"A young woman of ill repute is traveling on that train with Joe and a local miner. I have it on good authority that the lady is heading north, possibly to Oregon. However, she is suspect in a crime and is supposed to remain in my custody until the date of the trial. If you would be so good as to bring her back to me" – he pulled out some bills with a nonchalant air – "I will make it well worth your while. I would go after her myself, but I have more important business to attend to here."

The one with the beard shot a filthy hand out, but the other man asked with skepticism, "Don't we need to be deputized afore we go huntin' criminals?"

Rufus loosed a hearty laugh. "Boys, you have much higher hopes for this godforsaken country west of the Mississippi than anyone else in this mining town." Looking them both straight in the eyes, he added, "No, gentlemen. If we expect the law to be enforced here, we need to take it into our own hands."

He counted out some of the bills slowly, patiently. The

bearded man practically bounced on his toes, while the other stood as still as a support beam in a mine shaft, perhaps afraid to move and watch his dreams crumble beyond reach. Rufus smirked, enjoying the feeling of finally being the one to have all his dreams in hand. Well, almost all…

He pressed the cash into the bearded man's hand. "When you bring Sally Clay back here to me – alive – then I will double that amount. Do we have an understanding?"

Both men nodded, the money soothing all their doubts away, as Rufus knew it would. They rushed to the train station, the bearded man elbowing past others in line and the other never taking his gaze from the bearded man's money-stuffed hand.

He smiled as he turned away from the ridiculous scene. He should never have let himself become so dependent on just one woman to satisfy him, but no matter. She *would* be his.

Chapter 2

CALIFORNIA LOOKED LIKE GOLD as it sped by the window of the train. The summer-warmed hills of the interior might seem dry and barren to some, but to Sally the tan interspersed with some light green spoke of promise. A desire to begin anew rushed up from her heart, but it was a foolish notion. She would never break free from the sins of her past, nor would she be able to find peace until she confronted the reason she was out here in this beautiful but savage land in the first place. The admission caused an ache so deep she was sure she felt it in her bones.

"It's nice to get out of the Nevada desert, isn't it?"

She glanced over at Joe, but he just stared out the window, and she wondered if he had even uttered the question. The words sounded hopeful, but she could tell they were hollow inside, empty of life. For what reason, she could never guess. Nor did she want to try.

"Here." The man named Myghal handed her his tattered coat.

She shook her head. "I don't need it. I'm not cold."

"It's not for the cold."

Her hand went to her neck, then slid down to where her fingers brushed her collar bone. She squinted up at him through her long lashes and smiled – a slow, seductive smirk that came as naturally to her now as her girlish giggles used to do. "My dress bother you, Myghal?"

He shrugged his bony shoulders, unblinking. "No, ma'am, but I think it's drawing unnecessary attention."

Not bothering to acknowledge the leering gazes aimed her

way, she tilted her head and chuckled. "Maybe I like attention."
He would never know that she was once a shy, albeit determined, girl who only craved the attention of one man.

"Well, humor me, will ya?" He leaned forward and placed
the coat around her shoulders.

His gentle touch and the protective gesture confused her.
This was the same miner who had dumped a pitcher of water
on her when she'd tried to comfort a dark-haired, lonely man in
the only way she knew how anymore. The man had appeared so
lost as he downed his whiskey, speaking angrily with her boss
but obviously searching for a distraction to whatever was causing his eyes to glisten in the low light of the barroom. In that
moment she had felt a kinship with him that she didn't want to
let go. But Myghal had stopped them cold with a splash of water and taken the dark-haired man away, leaving her in that awful room, drenched and alone. So very, very alone.

Tears came to her eyes unbidden. While she had learned
long ago to cry whenever the act was needed, this was different.
She didn't want to cry.

Compassion softened Joe's face as she brushed a hand
across her eyes. Standing abruptly and buttoning the coat, she
pushed into the aisle and said over her shoulder, "I just need
some fresh air."

Making her way through the aisle was harder than she
thought. The jeers, whistles, and sniffs of disdain made her feel
like a criminal on her way to the gallows. But she held her head
high like Annabelle had taught her.

She could still hear Annabelle's words, soulful and beautiful like the sounds of the violin her daddy used to play.

*Don't let them intimidate you, Sally. They don't know what
you've been through. And don't for even one moment believe that
there is no hope. If a woman like me can get married and live a
decent life, so can you.*

Despite the comfort of the words, Sally couldn't take them to heart. She knew what Annabelle's marriage was like – how she was still treated like an outcast by society and how her own husband neglected her when she needed him most. It would be the same fate for Sally if she were to get married.

Swallowing back more tears, she walked out of the train car and stood on the small platform between it and the next car, leaning her arms against the railing and letting the wind run its fingers through her hair. The wind was her friend – its moaning and freezing force a kindred spirit many a long night.

She unbuttoned the top buttons of Myghal's coat and reached for the coin purse tucked in the lacy dip of her dress, warming her heart. For a moment, she simply closed her eyes as she held it, letting the dreams of the past crowd out the horrors of the present.

She recalled Jack's handsome face – the way his dusty brown hair hung roguishly over his kind, warm eyes. A smile lit his whole boyish face when he spoke of the West, and when he held her back home, it felt like a sunny day would surround her forever.

Hot tears pooled in her eyes at the intense longing that still flooded her at the thought of what once had been. Why couldn't he have been content in the promise of the life they could have shared? In her desperation, she thought that perhaps she would willingly suffer through these past three years again if it meant a future with him. Just maybe...

Watching her from the window, Joe could see how Sally could weave a spell over a man and make him fall for her – hard. With the wind toying with her sunbeam-hair, and a soft smile inviting a man to kiss away all her doubts, she looked vulnerable, and yet so happy, as if some wonderful dream could make her forget her present circumstances.

As he walked out to join her, the boards creaked beneath him, betraying his presence. The train swayed, and the background passed in a blur behind Sally as she turned her startled gaze to him. Upon recognition, her eyes grew cold and her posture stiffened. Joe found that he missed the softer blue of her eyes, before the realization of the interruption froze on her features.

"What do ya want, Joe?"

He knew he shouldn't ask, but he couldn't stop the words from leaving his mouth. "What were you thinkin' about just now?"

She paused, fiddling with some little pouch in her hands. "Nothing of any importance."

In that moment, she seemed regal. He couldn't exactly pinpoint why that word should whisper across his mind, but it somehow fit.

He started to reach out to still her fingers, which continued to clasp and unclasp whatever she was clutching, but he stopped himself before he got too close. Instead, he reached up and ran his hand through his hair, trying not to dwell on the thought of how nice it would be to run his fingers through hers.

He cleared his throat, nervous at the direction of his mind's wanderings. "It must have been something important to you if it put a smile the size of the Nevada desert across yer face." His voice dropped as he added gently, "You have a real nice smile, Sally."

Frowning, she tightened her hand over the pouch and shoved past him back into the passenger car. "Don't get used to it."

And the spell was broken.

Chapter 3

"I GUESS THIS is where we part ways."

They had barely set foot on the dock at Humboldt Bay before Joe tried shaking her off his boots like so much mud. Sally hated the fear that started weaving a web around her heart. She didn't need anyone, but the thought of separating from Joe and Myghal at this moment terrified her.

A shadow seemed to follow her all the way from Nevada – on the train ride from Reno to San Francisco, and on the three-day voyage by ship along the coast from San Francisco Bay to Humboldt Bay – and she was sure someone had been watching her the whole time. The feeling was unnerving, and while she longed to head to Oregon, she longed even more for companionship, at least for now. Plus, she needed more money before she could follow through with her plan. *But how to convince Joe to let me come with him?*

Sally's hand went to her chest, longing to grip the little coin purse full of comforting memories that lay close to her heart.

"You know, you never did tell me what exactly you and Myghal are doing in this part of California."

Joe's golden eyebrows lowered skeptically, while Myghal answered, "I got a letter from a friend o' mine talkin' 'bout this new town where we could maybe find some work loggin' the redwoods on the California coast. Pay's not too bad, and it sure beats minin'."

A wide smile showed the truth of his statement. Having met quite a few miners in the course of her time in Virginia City, she would have to agree. Surely anything beat mining, or any other work to be found in that horrid mining town.

She stepped out of the way of another passenger striding with purpose toward Eureka, gripping Joe's arm to steady herself. She winced when he shrugged her off, then followed at a respectable distance when he and Myghal began walking down the pier.

Eventually, she called out above the sounds of the slurping tide and the busy sailors, "What's the name of the town?"

"Falk."

"How long will you be stayin' out there?"

"Can't say fer sure yet."

"Are there women there, too?"

Her question was met with surprise and confusion on their faces as they both glanced back at her, and she realized that in her desperation to prolong their departure, she had shown her hand. Pulling out a handkerchief a young miner had given her once as a token of his "lasting" devotion, she wiped her brow in an effort to regain control of her emotions, but she couldn't stop her lips from trembling.

"I-I was wondering if perhaps…perhaps I might…see this town for myself. I'm decent at cooking, and I really need…some money."

Their silence following her words was even more awkward than her stuttered declaration. They stopped before stepping onto the street, but she refused to look at them as she waited. Her eyes fluttered to the shops, to the foggy sky, to the bay, to anything and everything but the rejection she felt sure was coming. After all, rejection always came to her.

"Well, I don't see why ye can't come along with us and see."

When she finally met Myghal's gaze, she could see uncertainty glimmering there – or perhaps it was the way he crossed and uncrossed his arms that made it so clear. But his words offered her hope, and she released the breath she had been holding. Then her gaze jumped to Joe, and the sight of his clenched jaw made her quickly gulp her breath back in.

"Sally, what's yer game? The deal was that you could travel with us, not follow us like a stray pup."

She gasped and took a step forward, ready to slap that contrary face of his and make him take back his words. When she raised her hand, Joe caught her wrist and grasped it hard.

"Don't even think about it."

She glared at his big hand swallowing her wrist. Before he could read her next intention, she kicked him in the shin with her fancy shoe. He swore and dropped her hand, rubbing his leg with a force he probably wished he could employ with her. A toss of her hair and a sweet smile caused him to rub at his leg even harder.

"Come now, yer mother taught ye better than that." Sally had no idea whether Myghal was referring to her or to Joe. Stepping between them, he added, "Sally's a lady, not a dog. And if she needs some help findin' work and a way to get back on her feet, then I say we should help her. That's what me own mother would want me to do. How 'bout you, Joe?"

Joe muttered but offered no discernible protest. He was too busy glaring at her with all the hostility he must have saved up ever since they left Virginia City. Not wanting to give Myghal a chance to see how un-lady like she really was, she did her best to wipe away her smile and take on the role of the injured party, complete with a watery gaze.

"Then it's settled. Falk is callin' my name, so let's get movin'." With that Myghal picked up the bag he had set down, took Sally's from her grasp, and headed into Eureka to find the stagecoach.

Please God, Sally's heart cried as she hurried after Myghal. She had no idea how to finish the plea.

Joe groaned, fed up with the injustices of life just as much as he was fed up with the jarring bounce of the stagecoach ride. He detested sitting across from Sally, watching her long blond hair rise and fall with the jerky movements of the wheels bouncing over the uneven ground. But apparently he wasn't the only one dealing with anger – Sally hadn't stopped glaring at him since he made the mistake of calling her a stray pup. He grunted and jerked his gaze out the window. He didn't regret it. He only wished that she had taken the hint and left him and Myghal alone.

Next to him, Myghal cleared his throat and nudged Joe hard in the side. "You two are worse than a couple o' dogs in a bettin' fight."

"Stop callin' me a dog!" Sally retorted with a huff before Joe could respond.

Myghal grinned, but Joe just shook his head. "If you'd stop behavin' like an animal, we'd be obliged to stop callin' you one."

If it didn't take all of one's strength to simply remain seated inside the stagecoach, he was pretty sure she would have reached over and strangled him. Despite his better judgment, a smile crept onto his face.

Sally sniffed and turned to look out at the passing scenery. He wished he could appreciate the grand trees and the coastal atmosphere, as well, but his belly grumbled with the emotions tumbling around inside him. Like a man seeing an abused stray, Sally's demeanor had made him cave in and take her along to California. But it wouldn't be long before she lashed out at the hand that helped her and took off with some other abuser. He wouldn't let himself get attached. No one else would ever have the opportunity to run off with his heart.

As soon as Sally reached down to let Myghal help her from the stagecoach, she realized her mistake. The handful of townsmen who weren't out working in the woods had turned curious gazes to the newcomers. Curiosity turned to surprise, and perhaps pleasure, when they saw her in her tattered, flashy red dress. She hadn't found an opportunity or the means to obtain a decent dress, and now her past would define her in this new place.

Glancing at Joe, she realized he wasn't even looking in her direction. Tossing her blond hair, she stepped primly down from the stagecoach, letting Myghal support her. But it wasn't the stability of his hand so much as the guilty compassion written on his gentle features that comforted her.

As her feet touched the ground, he whispered in her ear, "I'm sorry, Sally. I should've thought to get ye another dress."

"It isn't yer fault." Looking all around her, she leveled a glare at each man until he went back to whatever task he had been doing. No need for them to think she was still that kind of woman. If she could just get to Oregon and find Jack, perhaps she wouldn't ever have to be that woman again. Although she still wanted him to see what he had forced her to become.

"Want me to go with ya to the cookhouse?"

"No. I can handle myself just fine. You and Joe go see to yer own business."

He looked skeptical but headed off to find the owner, Noah Falk, anyway, with Joe marching ahead without a backward glance. *Aggravating man!*

Clasping Myghal's coat tight across her low-cut dress, she made her way to the cookhouse – or at least the building that smelled like a cookhouse. She had no idea if she was supposed to go see Noah Falk first like the boys were doing, but she figured she'd have a better shot with the cook, especially if she was given the chance to demonstrate the practical skills her mother had, once upon a time, passed down to her.

Head high and shoulders back, she pushed through the door and marched past the tables empty of people but full of dirty dishes. Following her nose to the kitchen, she stood in the doorway until the man bending over the stove turned and noticed her.

"Well, it's finally happened," he noted without much warmth as his dark eyes assessed her. He was powdered with flour, and a smidgen of butter or grease dripped from his rather muscular forearm. His tall frame would probably be better fitted for working alongside the men in the woods, but Sally figured he must possess some talent since the place smelled so inviting.

The cook picked up a well-used towel and rubbed his hands and arms with it. "I'll admit to some surprise at Noah allowing a woman like you here. He's a mite strict about that sort of thing."

A woman like you. Sally's neck ached with the strain of holding her head up, but she refused to look down at her shoes in shame. "I'm sorry, sir, but you're mistaken. I'm not that kind of woman." *Not anymore. Not here.*

The cook snorted and glanced pointedly at her dress. "Could've fooled me."

"I'm here to see if you could use an extra hand in the kitchen."

He turned away from her to plunge his hands in the washbasin, rinsing some of the piled-up dishes and taking his time before responding. "I could use an extra hand. You know how to cook?"

Sally jerked in surprise, causing her neck to pop. Wincing, she rubbed it and stuttered, "Y-Yes, sir."

"Mind you, I'd probably hire you right on the spot if all you could do was wash dishes." Peering over his shoulder, he added, "It's quite possible that's all you can do."

Sally inched toward the door leading to the dining hall. "Let me help you with dinner. Then you can decide if I'm worth my salt."

"It's not my place to hire anyone. But I reckon if you pass muster, I'll see that you get a job."

A sigh of relief escaped her lips, and she rushed the remaining few steps to the door.

"Where you goin'?"

Turning back to the growling man, she replied, "To gather the remaining dishes, of course."

She couldn't help the smile that grew on her face as she hurried to prove herself indispensible.

Chapter 4

HE WAS HERE.

It was a strange sensation, this knowing. Sally paid no attention to the woodsmen wandering about the logging town. No one questioned her as she hurried past the general store and the lumber mill, not even when she began running toward the forest. Fallers and choppers shouted back and forth to each other the farther into the woods she went, but no one shouted at her. The only voice she listened for was his.

And then she saw him. All other faces, all of her surroundings, were a blur as she focused on his handsome frame standing bold as brass amid the organized frenzy. He wasn't dressed like a logger. In fact, he looked just as she had last seen him – boyish cap from a trip to New England, the soft green shirt his mother had sewn him, brown britches, and those manly boots that made him appear even more confident than he was back in Missouri. Her breath caught at the sight of him. He was smiling at her – *smiling* – and all of her plans faded away in the force of his welcoming gaze.

She took one step forward, and still he waited, his teasing grin daring her to run to him. But just as she took another step, she noticed something literally looming over him. Belatedly, she heard the call, "TIMBER!"

Fear and cold sweat poured over her as she traced the path of that huge tree. It would crush him. With a terrified cry, she started running, running, running, but he never seemed to be any closer. Why wouldn't he move?

Suddenly, an arm wrapped firmly around her waist. She fought with all she had in her, sobbing hysterically, knowing that every moment she was held back was one less moment to reach him.

"Let me go!"

Then she blinked. Jack was gone, and it was night.

"Sally Clay, what in the world are you doing out here, shrieking like a banshee and running wild past the bachelors' quarters?"

Joe didn't release her, even when he felt her go limp in his arms.

She lifted her head weakly to peer back at him. "Where am I?"

"As if you don't know. I thought you were through with that kind of life, yet here you are practically begging the men to fall upon you. Don't you realize that I could have been anyone – *anyone?*" He was whispering fiercely in her ear, trying to get his own heartbeat to calm down, even as he could feel Sally's beating at a frightening pace against him.

"Joe, I..." She pushed away from him and spoke, just loud enough for him to hear, "I didn't know. I thought..."

Running a hand through his hair and glancing about to make sure no one was nearby, he sighed. "Sally, look at me."

She turned then, and Joe's heart melted. Tears coursed down her soft face, and she looked for all the world like a lost little girl who'd just had a nightmare. He stiffened. "Do you walk in your sleep?"

She swallowed hard and turned away again. "Sometimes.

Sometimes my dreams are so real, and when I wake up I'm no longer in my room." Tears rolled off her quivering chin.

"Aw, Sally." He held his hand out to her, but she didn't even look at him as she tucked her chin lower. He retracted.

Rubbing his arms to ward off the foggy chill, he suddenly wished he'd thought to bring a jacket. He cast another look behind him. He wouldn't tell Sally, but someone else had been following her. He hadn't been able to sleep, so when he heard her outside the room he shared with several other men, he quickly got up to investigate. It had scared him to see her running for the woods, a man shadowing her flight. But the man ran off in another direction as soon as he saw Joe, and Joe's biggest concern was to see to the hysterical Sally, who was well on her way to waking up the whole town.

With one last glance over his shoulder, he took a step toward her. "What were you dreaming about?"

She shook her head, her lips pressed tight.

He took another step closer. "My brother Seth used to move about in his sleep. He'd leave the ranch house and wander around outside. I always wondered what sort of dreams caused him to slip out of bed like that without realizing it."

With a sniff, she turned back to him. He could barely see her face in the moonlight, but he could tell by her posture and the tilt of her head that she had resolved not to reveal whatever dream had plagued her sleep.

She was so close he could have reached down and wrapped her in his arms. Resisting the urge, he instead crossed them tightly over his chest. "Don't you ever get tired of hiding your heart?"

"Since when have you encouraged me to share it with you?" She hitched her skirt and stalked off toward the home she now shared with a couple of other women who worked at the camp.

Without a word he walked behind her, determined to see her safely back to the house and make sure no one bothered her the rest of the night.

The dream haunted Sally as she made her way to the cookhouse the next morning for her first official day of work. The terror of knowing that Jack would be killed, gone forever, still nipped at her heels and prickled her skin. What if he were already dead? What if her dream were her heart's way of knowing that she would never see him again? The tears that had choked her last night rose up again in her eyes, and she tried to blink them away. It was this dad-blasted fog! No one could be happy when surrounded by this cold, gray mass.

No woodsmen were yet in the dining hall, a fact for which Sally was grateful. Before she entered through the kitchen door, she rubbed the tears away from her eyes and pinched her cheeks. The cook would have no reason to ask her personal questions today.

Stepping through the door, she waited for him to notice her. After a moment, he poked his head up from where he was bent over a mixing bowl. "You can get started on the bacon."

Then he turned back without another glance her way. So much the better.

Preparing the skillet, she tried to push away dark memories, but last night's dream brought some unwanted baggage that she couldn't seem to shake. Jack looked just the same in her dream as he had the last time she'd seen him, but there had been no smile then. Not for her.

"I know some of the men like the bacon burnt, but it's going to shrivel up to nothingness if you don't do something soon."

Startled, Sally quickly flipped the strips of bacon and got out a plate to set them on. She refused to give the cook the satisfaction of seeing her fail her first day on the job.

He hadn't failed. Joe had stayed up most of the night watching over Sally's new home, making sure she didn't wander out and no one else wandered in. The sleepwalking business worried him, along with the nagging feeling that someone else had been watching Sally, too.

Bone-tired and half-starved, he made his way to the cookhouse along with dozens of other men, most of them older, and all far more cheerful than they should be at this early hour, with a full day of work ahead. He found a seat beside Myghal on a rough-hewn log bench. A good number of benches filled the room and hugged either side of the long, scarred wooden tables.

Then Sally whisked in from the kitchen, and, though the conversations didn't die out, they certainly quieted as eyes took in her graceful form. She was wearing a different dress today – probably for the best – that made her resemble the neighborhood gal all the ranch hands used to fight over back in Nevada. Weren't too many of those respectable gals there, and there certainly weren't many in this California logging town. Made her all the more attractive, although Sally needed little help in turning heads.

Her bright smile and flirtatious banter had the men practically falling over themselves to converse with her before she floated back into the kitchen. It bothered Joe, although he hated himself for letting it get to him. Sally knew all about men and how to attract them. He couldn't forget her previous experience.

Myghal nudged him, following the action with a wink. "She sure didn't need our help in finding herself a job, did she?

Now that the men 'ave seen her, there's no way she'll be goin' anywhere anytime soon."

The smug, knowing look on Myghal's face made Joe tense up inside. "Wipe that smile off your face and pass me the butter."

Myghal obeyed the latter order but ignored the first. "Ya know, I think there's to be a dance in a few days. Every Saturday night they've got somethin' goin' on o'er at the dance hall. I'm aimin' to see if I can borrow me a fiddle and join in the fun."

Joe made no comment. All he could think about was Sally dancing with this rowdy bunch of men.

Myghal tipped his head to Joe's plate. "Well, best be finishin' up there. We've got a long day ahead of us."

And yet Myghal's silly grin remained as he slapped Joe on the back and took one last bite of breakfast.

"You fellas the new choppers?" one of the men asked before Joe could swallow his last mouthful and stand.

Joe nodded.

The man pushed back from the table. "You missed yer train. Those of us who work the mill eat here. The rest of you boys eat breakfast at the camp where you'll be workin'. The train leaves every mornin' at five."

Great. He and Myghal had already messed things up the first day on the job.

A long day indeed.

"You know, I don't know your name."

Sally plunged her hands into the lukewarm, soapy dishwater and waited, wondering if the cook would address her comment. This man – strong and yet silent if ever a man was – didn't engage in conversation very often. Her first encounter with him must have caught him off guard, because ever since he expected the both of them to work in silence and leave the other alone. Of course, it had only been one morning…but somehow Sally felt that this was the man's usual way. Distant or not, though, she ought to know his name.

"Zachary Taylor."

His matter-of-fact words spoken into their companionable quiet startled her, and she jerked her head up. "Zachary Taylor?"

He grunted.

Sally generally prided herself on not prying. She knew the pain brought about by someone asking too many questions. Still, she couldn't seem to stop herself as she scrubbed hard at a frying pan. "Is there a story behind that name?"

With a huff and an exasperated glance over his burly shoulder, he replied with his own question. "Isn't there always a story?"

That was far enough in Sally's mind. No need to learn his story, because she sure didn't want to feel obligated to return the favor. Instead, she concentrated on scrubbing pans and plates, then stacking them next to the basin. It had pleased her to see the satisfied men out there, their bellies full and smiles on their lips. And she wasn't so bothered by the flirting here, perhaps because she had a respectable job and the men were just having some harmless fun.

"My ma was from Mexico, and my pa was from the South."

Startled once again, Sally dropped a plate into the sudsy water, wrinkling her nose as she saw a damp spot form on her apron from the splash.

"My pa, John Taylor, fought in the Mexican War. I was born between the end of the war and Zachary Taylor's election in 1848."

Sally snuck a glance at the cook and caught him staring at the carrot he was holding, his hands motionless as he spoke. "If my pa knew what President Taylor would be like in office, he probably never would have named me Zachary after him. My pa always made sure I knew that I was named after Taylor before his presidency, when he was simply a war hero and not the man who betrayed the South with his ideas of bringing in new territories as free states."

Mr. Taylor returned to chopping the carrot as her own hand slowed its circling on the tin plate she held. It was the most he had said to her all morning. "You mean, like California?"

"Yep."

"What did yer ma think of all this?"

"Hated it. She fell in love with my pa, not the United States. In fact, she refused to call me Zachary. Called me Juan instead, since my pa wouldn't let her call him that."

Sally couldn't help a giggle at that. "What did yer pa do?"

"Nothing. I've always been a man with two names. But Juan was only my name as a child. My ma died when I was ten."

He quit talking, chopping off his words with the same force he used to dice vegetables, and Sally understood. The story was getting too personal, too painful. Why dredge up memories that hurt? She pondered this man who knew his way around a kitchen, once had another name, clearly loved his mother and somehow regarded his father, and managed to look formidable and innocent at the same time.

Suddenly, one of the mill workers strode into the kitchen. Sally had forgotten that one man was still eating when she had last gathered the dishes. The plate and utensils looked awkward in his rough hands, but he gave her a disarming smile as he handed them to her.

"Thought I would bring these to ya. Looks like the last o' them."

"Thank you."

The man lingered, shifting from one foot to the other and

keeping his gaze trained on her. Before he could open his mouth, though – which he seemed to think about doing once or twice – Mr. Taylor stated, "That will do."

He didn't turn from his spot across the kitchen preparing vegetables for dinner, but his tone held undeniable authority and a note of hostility. The other man made a quick disappearance.

With a smile, Sally realized that Zachary Taylor was a man who won battles.

Chapter 5

"LOOK AWAY, look away, look away…"

The words of the song swirled around him, but somehow Joe couldn't look away. He watched Sally as she danced with one of the men on his crew, twirling and shuffling with some moves he was sure he had never seen before. A smile crept up his face at the thought that perhaps she was making them up as she went along. But the smile fled when he realized how experienced she was and how many times she had danced in the past with filthy miners and the like. Men who had used her and never cared for her.

Why the men had allowed Zachary Taylor, one of the cooks, to sing a melancholy rendition of "Dixie" tonight was beyond Joe. The Civil War had ended over twenty years ago, and perhaps even further back in the minds of these young California men, but apparently they didn't mind the slower tune or the song of the South. Besides, a crowd had gathered in the dance hall, each hoping to have Sally handed off to them, so few of them cared about the music itself. A couple of other women were being swept across the rather dirty dance floor, but it was Sally that the single men wanted to hold and sway with. Joe clenched his jaw in frustration.

Taylor's deep voice faded, and the guitar-picking came to an end. Taking a deep breath, Joe determined to dance with Sally. Seeing her graceful form, there was no way he could walk away, let alone look away.

❁

Sally never tired of dancing. It was a joy, one of the few she had been able to claim over the last three years when horrid guilt and hate had filled most of her heart. Jack hadn't cared much for dancing, but he had obliged her a couple of times before he was lured away by the West.

Suddenly, Mr. Taylor's song ended, and Myghal stepped up with his fiddle, a huge grin on his slightly tanned face. Before she knew what was happening, she was in Joe's arms, and Myghal started up a fast-paced, albeit haunting tune. With sudden warmth she realized that Joe was a wonderful dancer. She felt secure as he gently guided her into each new spin and shuffle. A blessed sense of belonging filled her, so different from the feeling she got when dancing with that bearded logger just moments before.

Refusing to dwell on the man's leering grin or the way he had leaned in far too close to whisper in her ear, Sally released her anxiety and simply danced. Myghal's fiddling was magnificent, and soon she was smiling and laughing like she had back at home. If only she was home, and Jack was holding her…

Glancing up at Joe as he confidently maneuvered her across the floor and offered her a genuine smile, Sally found that she didn't mind being in his arms. She used to pretend, as much as possible, that the men she danced with in the saloons were all Jack, but not this time. Joe's happiness, something she hadn't seen since she asked him to take her to California, made her want to embrace the truth of his presence rather than the lie of Jack's.

Never had Joe seen such huge trees. Stories about the redwoods seemed more like fiction than fact – and yet here they were, taller than anything he would have ever pictured. There were other tall trees here, too. And he had to chop them down.

Standing on a springboard held in place by notches in the tree, Joe wondered if he didn't fear heights when he was younger because he'd never been up in a tree like this one before. One false move and…

"Stop lookin' down at the ground. Ain't gonna help ya none."

Joe grimaced and peered around the solid trunk at Myghal. "Thanks, but I could've figured that one out on my own."

Myghal leaned back, his red head resting on the redwood while he pulled a handkerchief out of his pocket to wipe away the sweat on his brow. His other hand sat lightly on the crosscut saw, looking for all the world like he was at home in this giant of a tree.

Finally, Joe grabbed onto his end of the saw again, and they resumed cutting into the tree. Back and forth. Back and forth. Back and forth. Just like Joe's thoughts regarding Sally.

Two nights ago, he had been proud to hold Sally in his arms. The radiance of her smile thrilled his heart, and he didn't think of Elizabeth once the whole evening. The beautiful sight of Sally dancing was enough to fill his mind – and then some. But now he wished that he could take it all back. Becoming attached to her was the last thing he needed. He had promised himself that no one would have a chance to break his heart again, and if there was one guarantee when it came to Sally, it was that someone's heart was bound to get broken.

Well, it won't be mine.

Memories of the dream that had been fluttering at the edges of her mind rushed back to the forefront of her thoughts at the *boom* of a tree falling somewhere in the forest.

Turning her attention back to the chicken she was preparing, Sally felt a tear begin to slide down her cheek.

Why can't Jack leave me alone? Isn't it enough that he crushed my heart? Must he keep coming back into my thoughts to stomp on the pieces?

She plucked the chicken with a fury, wishing she could pluck the pride and arrogance right out of Jack Harvey.

"What'd that chicken ever do to you?"

Despite her frustration, Sally couldn't help the smile that twitched at her lips. "Nothing."

"I'd hate to see what you're like when someone does do something to make you mad."

Mr. Taylor never looked up from the potatoes he was mashing. His movements were sure and purposeful. The man had plenty of confidence in the kitchen.

"Have you ever been in love, Mr. Taylor?"

His head lifted then. The intensity in his gaze surprised her, and she held her breath as she waited for his response.

"Nope." He added a splash of milk to his concoction and went back to mashing.

She doubted the veracity of his response, but decided not to push him. He would be likely to push her right back – and right out the door of his kitchen.

"*You* have, though," Mr. Taylor said with certainty, his dark eyebrows raised despite the fact that he was no longer looking at her.

"I don't see how that's any of yer business," she huffed.

"Neither is my love life any of yours."

There was a pause.

"How have you managed to keep from falling in love?" Sally whispered the question, wanting desperately to know his secret.

"I don't hang around women."

"None at all?"

"Not until you showed up. You rarely meet single women in the gold fields or in a lumber camp. A man can't rightly fall in love unless he meets a woman."

Sally twirled a chicken feather, watching it spin around and around, away from its rightful place. How might her life be different if she had never met Jack? If she had stayed at home with her family instead of running off to the dance hall in town, she might have been safe. But if she hadn't met Jack, she might never have come to the West. Would that have been a good thing?

"You can't always avoid meeting someone of the opposite sex," she finally replied. If it hadn't been Jack, it would certainly have been someone else.

"Perhaps not."

Trying to lighten the now somber mood in the kitchen, she smiled and injected a note of teasing in her tone. "It's probably best you avoid women, Mr. Taylor. Otherwise you'd be carrying around a string of broken hearts."

"You misjudge me, Miss Clay. I'm a cook. I don't break

things; I make things for people to enjoy."

The sincerity in his dark eyes caused her to look away, emotion catching in her throat.

Rufus O'Daniel fingered the handle of his sturdy, ornate roll-top desk, unable to concentrate on the paperwork in front of him because a certain golden-haired angel – or was it devil? – refused to leave his mind. He should have gone after her himself. Oh, but wouldn't all of his competitors and the other good-for-nothings in Virginia City just love to see him crawling after a whore like a lost little lamb. Silver was the shepherd around here, leading them all by the noses until the day it drove them straight off the nearest cliff.

Rufus pounded his fist on the covered desk. He hated the whole sorry business, but he still held to the notion that one day he would be the one to lead everyone else around – including Sally. For that was what love really was: not mutual affection, not abiding friendship, but one person being in control of the other. He had seen it with his own parents, along with enough other couples to have the idea hammered into him. It simply wasn't possible to find happiness in any relationship until he was the one with the upper hand.

Now he had to decide if having the upper hand with Sally meant hunting her down himself or waiting for her to fall into his snare.

Slamming the lid of the desk back, he searched for an address he had made note of long ago and stuffed in one of the desk's compartments. He swore when he was unable to find it, fingering a match in his pocket and momentarily contemplating burning the ridiculous piece of furniture to the ground. Instead, he snapped the match in two and stormed out of the office.

Chapter 6

A SHRILL SOUND came from somewhere outside the cabin, and in his weary state Joe couldn't tell if it was the whistle signaling the start to the work day or something else. Could it really be time to begin again? It felt like he had just crawled into bed. He peeled his eyes open painfully, the resistance causing him to tear up. Darkness still clung to the cabin, but that didn't mean anything around a lumber camp.

The other dozen or so men that fit into this pitiful excuse of a cabin looked to be out like wind across a candle. While Joe struggled to recall what awakened him, he heard it again. Weeping. After throwing on his pants, boots, and a tattered coat, he stumbled out the door as quietly as he could.

He knew it was her before he even saw the silhouette of her form on the edge of the tiny, sagging porch. For a moment, though, the only name that came to his mind was "Elizabeth." Holding her while she cried. Comforting her after David's betrayal. Hoping she would choose his arms forever.

"Sally." He touched her shoulder gently, but she didn't respond, except perhaps to cry harder. "I'll take you back to your cabin."

She jerked from his touch. "No!"

He cringed at her loud protest. Eventually, his luck would run out and one of the boys would join them. "Keep yer voice down," he whispered harshly.

She shook her head in exaggerated motions, her hair falling

into her face. "Stay away from me. I'll never belong to you. He'll come back for me. He will!" Flinging herself from the porch, she took off for the woods.

She was sleepwalking again – he could tell by the way she didn't meet his gaze.

"Not again," he muttered under his breath as he took off after her. At this rate, he'd be forced to recruit Myghal to take turns keeping watch over Sally's home all night, every night. The thought made him want to drop right where he was and sleep in blissful ignorance of the world and all of its problems.

Sally was remarkably fast, as if she truly thought she had to flee from him. What was she dreaming about? Joe pushed himself in his groggy state, but he still lost sight of her in the darkness.

"Sally!" He called her name as loudly as he dared, his heart pumping even faster at the silence that met his ears. He couldn't even hear her running anymore.

All of a sudden, the sounds of a scuffle originated somewhere off to his right. He couldn't seem to find traction on the wet leaves as he spun toward the noise, and he almost fell flat on his face as his legs attempted to stay ahead of his upper body. Then she was in his arms with so much force that it was as if someone had pushed her. The surprise sent him reeling backward, and, in a moment, he and Sally found themselves in a sorry pile of leaves and pine needles and mud.

"Joe?" Her voice was small, not her usual sassy or flirtatious tone.

Leveraging himself on his elbows, he turned toward her, where she was curled up on her side in the mire. "Yeah, it's me. Are ya hurt?"

She was weeping again, and the sound broke his heart. Against his better judgment, he gently eased her up from the ground and into his arms, rocking her back and forth as he stroked her tangled hair. As she cried against his shoulder, he wondered what he ought to do with this woman who promised to be the cause of many sleepless nights to come.

Shame. It surrounded her just as surely as Joe's arms did, making her feel dirty, stuck. What was wrong with her? Must Joe always find her at the moment she was falling apart? Although being in his comforting embrace made her wonder if she were still dreaming.

She had been running from Rufus O'Daniel, running from his claims that she would never see Jack again, that her only hope was to accept a life with him. Escape seemed so sure until she ran straight into him, his cruel, restraining hands ready to drag her away. But then...

Then he had pushed her away, straight into another man's arms – Joe's. That last part had been real, hadn't it? Because here she was in his protective arms.

What shamed her most at this moment was that she didn't want to pull away. She hadn't felt safe in such a long time. Choking on another sob, she buried her face in his shoulder and let him hold her.

When her tears finally started to dry, Joe stood up, hooking an arm beneath her legs and cradling her. She didn't protest as he held her securely against his chest. Chancing a glance up at his face, she caught his usual stubborn expression. Yet when he looked down at her, his eyebrows relaxed a bit and his mouth...

Oh. A strong urge to kiss him blew over her like a fierce wind.

He adjusted his grip as he carried her back toward the cabins, and she clung to him. His stride was sturdy, confident. This hardly seemed like the Joe she knew back in Virginia City –

the one who was lovesick and rather clueless when it came to women. This wasn't a boy parading as a man. Joe was now a man who had experienced heartache and somehow matured because of it.

All too soon they were at her place. Joe set her down slowly, but Sally didn't want to let go. She grasped his coat, meeting his gaze as he stood on the top step of the small porch.

"Joe, I…" But what could she say?

"Try to get some sleep, Sally. I'll have Myghal stay out here to make sure you'll be all right until morning."

He wasn't staying himself? Slowly unclenching her death grip on his coat, she stepped back and nodded once. To him she was a prisoner to be guarded, a guilty person who had to be watched so she didn't cause trouble in the camp.

Disgusted with herself, she shuffled into the cabin and pushed the door shut behind her, wishing she could slam it without waking the others.

Perhaps this was the catalyst she needed. It was time to do what she came to do. Joe wouldn't need to bother with her anymore.

Chapter 7

A WEEK HAD PASSED since her nighttime run-in with Joe and her dream of Rufus. This night's run was no dream, but if Joe saw her, she'd pretend to be sleepwalking and try again another night. She desperately hoped she had timed this right, though, as she longed to be on her way – on her own again, until she found Jack.

It scared her to realize how deeply her hopes rested on him.

She absently rubbed the coin purse in her hands, holding onto it for no other reason than that it always comforted her, reminding her of the Jack she used to know back home. Before he abandoned her. The *clink* of the items inside was like the first note of a song – a moment of promise.

Gathering her courage and her skirts, she brushed past Myghal. He had to be asleep, as he hadn't stirred from his position on the porch steps when she opened the door. His knees were tucked up to his chest, his arms folded on top of them and his head resting on his arms. He looked utterly exhausted, and how could she blame him? He and Joe had been taking turns sitting outside of her lodging every night, on top of all the hard work they did every day.

With one last glance at Myghal's bent form, she rushed through the sleeping town. She probably could have run off days ago, but she wanted to be sure it was a night when Joe wasn't guarding her and when Myghal would be dead tired.

And if she were honest, she was having a hard time motivating herself to leave this place where she had a decent job working for a good man. Her gaze, finally adjusted to the dark, brushed over the cookhouse. She hated to up and leave Zachary Taylor, but all she had to do was recall Jack's face to give her that one last push toward freedom from Joe's watchful eye.

Clutching the satchel stuffed with the few belongings she had collected since she left Virginia City, she made it past the last few buildings and took off running into the woods, grateful for the rain-soaked earth that silenced her footfalls.

She kept the train tracks in her sight, hoping they would lead her to Eureka, where the men transported the lumber and where she could get a few supplies for her northbound journey. Her sense of direction was useless at best, so she would have to seek out landmarks along the way, but she wouldn't let worry find a foothold in her heart. Every step she took at this point was a step toward Jack. If she could only find him, it didn't matter what he did. If he accepted her, she would finally find peace and joy. If he didn't, then she would make sure he would never be able to ignore her memory. She'd find a way to make sure that she would haunt his thoughts the rest of his life, just as he had been haunting hers.

Being ignored was her greatest fear and her biggest hurt. To have someone know she existed and then simply refuse to acknowledge her or care about her feelings…

Her thoughts flitted to her parents and the memory of how they'd doted on her younger siblings. And Jack – showering her with attention and then leaving her behind. Nothing ached like *that* pain.

Shoving her thoughts aside, she tried to focus on her breathing, which was becoming more labored. As soon as the tracks came into view, she stopped for a moment, huffing and puffing. She had been running like monsters from storybooks were after her. With a rueful smile, she decided that the memories that terrorized her were far scarier than any fictional creature, no matter how horrible.

Joe snuck out of the cabin before the whistle could rouse everyone for another never-ending work day. He wanted to check on Myghal and make sure the poor man had a chance to prepare himself for the day.

Slogging through the mud, he finally came upon the women's housing several minutes later. Everything appeared fine, except that Myghal looked like he'd been out cold for a while. Gripping his thin shoulders, he gave Myghal a quick shake and resisted the urge to yell, "Daylight in the swamp!" The thought of Myghal's likely reaction made him smile wide, though.

Lifting his head and stretching his long limbs, Myghal squinted up at him. "Mornin', Joe. What's put a smile on yer ugly face?"

Joe smirked and shook his head. "Just thinkin' up some fun ways to wake ya up next time."

"Thanks fer the warning." Myghal grinned as he slowly stood up.

"Any trouble last night?"

Myghal cupped a hand to his mouth, blew out, and grimaced. "Well, I can't say fer sure. To be honest, I don't remember a thing."

Despite a quick pulse of panic, Joe replied, "It would be nice if Sally had a peaceful night's rest for once." But he couldn't squelch the feeling that something was wrong.

"She must've, as there's no way I could sleep through her dream-walkin'."

They both looked to the little house, waiting. Sally always

woke before the whistle in order to help Taylor with breakfast. A few minutes went by, but no sounds rustled from the building. Joe sat down on the steps, trying to ignore the irrational fear churning in his gut. Maybe she had just slept in...

The door creaked open, and Joe jumped up next to Myghal. But it wasn't Sally. One of the other women stepped out onto the porch, gasping when she caught sight of them.

Glaring at them, she lowered her hand from her heart and then eased the door shut behind her. "What are you boys doin' out here?" she whispered harshly, crossing her arms over her chest.

Myghal spoke confidently and calmly. "We were jest waitin' fer Miss Sally so we could walk her to the cookhouse."

"Well, ya must have just missed her. She's not in her bed." Sweeping haughtily past them down the steps, she added, "Now if you'll excuse me, some of us have better things to do than laze about where we're not wanted." She took off in the direction of the general store.

The panic returned full force. Gripping Myghal's coat, Joe whispered, "Are you sure she didn't come out at all last night?"

Uncertainty filled Myghal's normally warm eyes. "I don't know. I don't remember hearing anythin'."

Before Myghal could stop him, Joe vaulted up onto the porch and swung open the door. A couple of women shrieked, but Joe paid them no mind as he scanned the room, rushing to the two empty beds, jerking off the covers, and pulling the drawers out of the small dressers nearby. Sally was gone, and it appeared her belongings were, as well.

Slamming the door shut behind him, he took off for the cookhouse, hoping that Sally had just been too quiet on her way to work to wake up Myghal. Of course, if she were there, he'd probably strangle her. *Please, God, let her be there!*

Bursting into the cookhouse, he made a beeline for the

kitchen. Dismay overtook him as he ran past empty benches and shot into the kitchen, where Taylor stood by himself, jumping at Joe's sudden appearance.

"What's going on?" Taylor looked startled, and a bit perturbed at having the solitude of his kitchen invaded.

Behind him, Joe heard Myghal's heavy footsteps pound through the doorway. "Have you seen Sally this mornin'?"

"No, but that's not unusual. She should be here any moment."

Ignoring the delicious smells of Taylor's cooking, Joe choked out, "She's gone."

Taylor's eyes darkened as he glared at Joe. "What do you mean she's gone? Where would she go?" He flung the towel he had been gripping onto a table. "What's goin' on?"

"Sally often walks in her sleep, so Myghal and I have been taking turns sitting outside her cabin every night. Myghal fell asleep during his watch last night, and now we can't find her."

"Aren't you boys overreacting? She could just be freshening up. She is, after all, a woman." He picked the towel back up and twisted it in his hands, making Joe think he might be more troubled than his words suggested.

Joe didn't have a response for that, so he simply stormed past Myghal and headed outside. He marched past the general store and glanced in every building he came across on the way out of the small town, hoping for a glimpse of Sally, but all was still dark and mainly undisturbed by human movements.

Myghal caught up to him again and clenched his fists. "I'm sorry, Joe. I thought fer sure I would've heard her leave."

A thought resounded through Joe's mind. "Unless...she didn't want you to hear her."

"Ya think she purposely ran off?"

"Yes."

"But where would she go?"

"Well, no matter where she wanted to go from here, she'd probably head for Eureka first, right?" Joe wished he could remember if Sally had said anything about any other destination she'd originally had in mind, but nothing came to him. Had he ever asked her?

"I suppose so."

"Let's go then."

Before he could sprint away again, Myghal grabbed his arm. "If we follow Sally, I doubt we'll be comin' back anytime soon."

"We'll make her come back."

Myghal raised his eyebrows at that. "I think we should be grabbin' our things."

"We'll just miss one day of work – and I'll make sure she doesn't forget that."

Myghal tightened his grip. "Joe, listen to me. Sally's a stubborn lass. Ye won't be convincin' her to come back unless it's what she wants. If yer serious about followin' her, yer going to haveta be willin' to give up this job. We're not settin' out to kidnap her – I won't be a part of that. We're going to help her get wherever she's so desperate to go, or we just let her go and keep workin' here."

Taking a deep breath, Joe let Myghal's words set his panicked thoughts in some kind of order. "Why would she leave, Myghal?"

"Guess she was jest ready to move on." Running a hand over his eyes and through his hair, he heaved a weary sigh.

Joe understood how he felt. They had a good thing going here. Was it really worthwhile to go chasing after a woman who clearly didn't want their help anymore? How had it come to this, anyway? Only a few weeks ago he would have been glad to see her going her own way – maybe.

He ground his boot into the dirt and searched the edge of

the dawn-lightened woods. "I have a bad feeling about leavin' her on her own. Someone here's been watching her – probably half the lumber camp, actually. She needs us." *I need her, too.* The thought chopped at his head with the force of a double-bitted axe.

Myghal headed to the cabin to gather their belongings and alert Mr. Falk of their departure – hopefully they would still get some pay for their time. Joe returned to the kitchen, planning on begging some food out of Taylor, but there was no need. When he pushed through the swinging door, Taylor met him with a sack of supplies. "I figured she wouldn't stay here very long. Something was bothering her that she'll have to face sooner or later. Perhaps this is for the best."

Joe nodded, uncertain how to respond.

"Will you tell her I'll miss her?"

Again Joe nodded, his heart and throat constricting. "I will."

It took much longer to get to Eureka than Sally had originally hoped. She had never been able to get new shoes, and the ones she was wearing were too thin and too fancy to be of much use. Her feet felt numb from the cold and the constant pressure against her toes.

Not to mention that she had hoped to get food in Eureka. As it was, the little money she had saved was doing her no good in the forest. The encroaching twilight was eating away all of her hope and energy, and, if it weren't for Jack's ghost alternately hounding her steps and taking her by the hand, she was sure she would have given up and turned back hours ago.

The tracks she had been staring at the whole day began to blur as tears and weariness clouded her vision. Was this what it was going to be like all the way to Oregon?

As she pushed on, a sudden chill overtook her. Jack's ghost seemed to have company, as she felt certain she was being watched, despite the fact that she couldn't see anything behind her. Veering off to the left, she moved away from the railroad tracks and deeper into the forest, trying to keep to the shadows of the overlarge trees.

Nothing stirred, but still she waited, hating the darkness that permeated the sky. She hadn't planned on being stuck out in the woods at night. She felt so weak, so cold, and so much like the sheltered little girl Jack had assumed her to be that day he abandoned her.

Sinking down into the sorrel and dirt at the base of the nearest tree, she gave into the memory she couldn't ever seem to hide from for long.

"Jack! Jack! Wait for me!" She took off after him, excited about the future she had tracked down to this very dusty mining town. His head came up at the sound of his name, and then he turned slowly and met her gaze.

"Sally?"

His cap hid his eyes, and she shoved through the crowd departing the train station as quickly as possible, not wanting to miss his surprise and delight. She had made a way for them to be together, sneaking away from her parents' refusal to see reason. Wouldn't Jack be so grateful for her sacrifice?

"I'm here, Jack!" She hastened to stand in front of him, looking up with all the adoration and commitment she could muster.

He was silent for a while, and she began to fidget beneath his unreadable gaze. "Aren't you pleased?"

"What are you doing here?" They weren't the first words she had wished from his mouth, but maybe he was just too overcome with shock at her unexpected presence.

"I took the train, too. I purposely didn't let you see me 'cause I wanted to surprise you." But what had seemed like such innocent

fun on the train now seemed ridiculous in light of the condescension in his green eyes — those beautiful green eyes that matched his nice green shirt so perfectly. If only he was looking at her with the love she had been craving during the long trip.

Instead of sweeping her into his arms, he gripped her shoulders tightly. "Sally, you shouldn't be here. You don't belong in a place like this. Go home."

He started to turn away, and panic flared in her chest. She latched onto his elbow. "I do belong here — with you. I'll help you make a home where you'll be comfortable. Goodness knows you need a wife and a house in this uncivilized wilderness if you hope to survive." She injected a bit of humor into her tone, but that smile she had fallen in love with was nowhere to be seen.

"We already said our good-byes. I'm starting over out here." He must have noticed her eyes filling with tears, because he added, "I'm sorry. I never wanted to hurt you, but you know I'm not ready to settle down. I left to find adventure, and maybe some silver while I'm at it." Then he smiled, and she almost believed it was going to be all right.

"I won't interfere, Jack — you know I won't. You can do whatever you want. Please, just let me share some of those adventures with you." Back home, she had felt so confident in his attention, and those memories made her hate this begging, pathetic side of her that was taking over.

His sweet smile turned into one full of pity as he repeated, "Go on home, Sally." It was just as if he were commanding a stray dog. Then he turned and melted into the crowd.

"Jack!" Full-fledged panic gripped her and stole her heart away. She didn't have enough money to go back home, and even if she did, how could she face her family and friends after being rejected like this? "Jack!"

She called his name again and again, but he had disappeared. She had never expected him to refuse her, not even in her worst *nightmares. He had seemed so reluctant to leave her behind that she was sure he would be glad she had followed him.*

But he wasn't glad. He didn't care for her at all.

Tipping her head back against the bark of the tree, she let a few tears fall. How horrible that first night had been. The cemetery where she had slept had seemed to symbolize all her dead plans and hopes. For days she'd wandered the town trying to find him, but she eventually realized that he didn't want to be found. A saloon- and brothel-owner named Jacob found her half-starved and half-asleep on the wooden sidewalk one night and offered her a job. With no other options and all of her money spent buying that one-way train ticket, where else was she to go? What else was there for her in that dreadful mining town?

As the bitter memories seeped through her, she knew there had been another part of her that embraced the work, at least at first. Jack had crushed her self-respect, and she craved the sense of belonging as one of Jacob's girls. All too soon, though, she'd recognized that the life of a soiled dove only alienated her from the world and the person she used to be – as well as the person she had always wanted to become. She was always lonely, but she had never had the courage or confidence to escape until she caught wind of Jack's whereabouts from a needy miner and ran from one man while trailing after two others.

"Must my self-worth always be determined by men?" she whispered into the bleak night. All she heard was the cry of an owl, repeating over and over again, "Who? Who? Who?"

Chapter 8

THE FOG AND COLD seemed dreadfully out of place in this summer night, but Sally had to keep reminding herself that she was no longer in Nevada, or even in Missouri. She was on the North Coast of California, among the mighty redwood trees that comforted her and terrified her all at once with their height and solid strength.

She told herself to get up off the ground but couldn't seem to find the energy. Night had fully descended upon the forest, and she didn't think she could find the railroad tracks even if she wanted to. So she sat on the forest floor, wavering in and out of consciousness as she dreamed of sagebrush and river boats, Joe and Jack.

Voices suddenly penetrated her lethargy, and, in a moment, she was fully awake and standing by the tree, trying in vain to see where they were coming from. It sounded like two men having a conversation. Part of her longed to call out and see if maybe they could direct her to Eureka, but, as soon as she opened her mouth, her fear kept any sound from emerging. Could she really take such a dreadful risk?

The voices stopped, and the opportunity seemed to have passed. Head in her hands, she sank back down to the ground and gave in to her weariness.

Before long, though, she heard footfalls not far from where she sat. She stiffened, heart beating fast as she squinted in an effort to see who might be close by. Finally, she made out a tall, thin silhouette walking past, and her heart sped up with her desire to ask for help. Tears burning her eyes, she threw caution aside and whispered, "Wait." Then, more loudly, "Wait!"

Jack! Wait for me! I'm here...

The silhouette stopped, an apparition that seemed to appear and disappear as it blended in with the shadows. Then it sped toward her, running and calling her name. "Sally! Can ye hear me? Where are ya?"

Myghal. Intense relief clutched her heart and brought more tears to her eyes. "I'm here."

He skidded to a stop, then knelt in front of her. "We wasn't sure we would ever find ye. Thank goodness yer all right, lass." His hybrid accent was heavier and stranger than normal, and it made Sally want to laugh. But when she opened her mouth, sobs burst out instead.

Myghal took her hands in his as if to help her stand, but concern covered his face as he held on. "How long have ye been sittin' here? Your hands are froze clear through." Sandwiching them between his, he began to rub gently. She gasped with the sudden warmth that filled her and then closed her eyes, relishing the moment of safety.

Finding Sally in this dark night would be like finding silver in the mines after they had been played out, especially since she didn't seem to want to be found. Joe was seething, frustrated that Sally's whims were taking him farther and farther from the life he had imagined for himself.

I'm sick of these games. Women are nothing but trouble.

"Joe!"

He turned at the sound of his name. After hearing a couple more calls, he settled on a general direction and started running. Roots and broken branches scraped his boots. He managed to stay on his feet, but when he caught sight of Sally, pale and shivering as she sat beneath a giant redwood tree surrounded by ferns, he dropped his bag and went straight to his knees.

"Sally, are ya all right?" He gently took one of her small hands in his while Myghal continued rubbing warmth into the other. She was a queen with her golden hair framing her sweet face, eyes closed as she allowed her devoted servants to assist her. For the moment, Joe didn't mind being a servant if it meant slowing the silent tears leaking down Sally's cheeks. He wished she would say something – he ached to hear her voice.

"Sally?"

She sniffed and tucked her head to her shoulder. "I'm so glad you found me." Her voice broke as she whispered the muffled words.

"What were ya doin' just sittin' here?" It wasn't like her to just give up...or was it? Did he really know her that well?

She wouldn't meet his gaze as she tried to tug her hands back from him and Myghal. But they both held on, and her head snapped up, a bit of fire mixing with the water still in her eyes. "Let me go."

"Are ye hurt?" Myghal's question was soft, patient.

"No." She bit her lip, and Joe couldn't explain the warmth that suddenly spread through his limbs. "But my feet..."

"What's wrong with yer feet?" Had she twisted something? Broken something?

"Nothing." Bestowing a glare upon him, she concluded, "They're just cold and hurting."

Dropping her hand, he scooted back, then grabbed one of her feet.

"I'm fine – leave it alone."

"Didn't ya ever get different shoes? These are useless out here."

"Don't ya think I'm aware of that now?"

An unstoppable smile broke out at her petulant gaze. Turning his attention back to her feet, he slipped off her ridiculous shoes and her soaked stockings.

"Joe, my feet are freezing!"

"Well, damp stockings aren't going to help ya any." The smile disappeared – he didn't have the patience to force it to stay.

"Please. I'm cold." Her voice came out as a whimper as she drew her feet underneath her dress.

"Sally, I'm not goin' to make you walk around with bare feet. You're goin' to wear a pair of my socks, and we're goin' to make camp here for the night while our things dry out." He rummaged in his bag for his extra pair of socks as he continued, "Tomorrow we're headin' to Eureka, where our first stop will be a mercantile so we can get you some decent clothing." He pretended not to notice her flinch at the word "decent," but he wished he could take it back. Sally didn't need to have her past always rubbed in her face.

"Our things will never dry out here."

Myghal chuckled, but since she sounded so close to tears again, Joe chose not to respond. Instead, he held out a sock expectantly, waiting for her to allow him to help her. She looked ready to defy him, but a shiver shook her resolve, and she slowly extended her leg. They both seemed to gulp air at the same time as he touched her delicate foot.

Sally's shivering increased at the warm, firm touch of Joe's hand on her foot. Grasping her ankle, he slowly covered her foot with the sock, then rubbed it for a moment. She offered him her other foot, and he repeated the comforting procedure. Her heart warmed, and she wished he would never let go. She belonged here.

I do belong here – with you!

Wincing, she shook her head. She had been wrong before. Maybe she didn't know where she belonged.

Joe and Myghal stood.

"I brought an extra bedroll," Myghal noted. He grinned, then he and Joe went about clearing a space for a small fire and their bedrolls while Sally watched, feeling pathetic and helpless and exhausted…

A while later – she didn't know how long she had been sleeping against the tree – someone picked her up and helped her get into a bedroll.

"Don't leave," she whispered.

Joe's steady voice drifted back to her. "I'm not leavin', Sally."

Reassured, she curled up on her side and went back to sleep.

Chapter 9

SLEEP HAD ELUDED Rufus all night long, and nothing – no one – could satisfy his restlessness. No one except for a certain golden-haired minx who was too far away to be of any assistance.

He leaned back in his chair, staring at the telegram on top of his desk. He had fed on local gossip at the Washoe Club and finally discovered that Joe Clifton and his Cornish miner-friend had been heading for Falk, a lumber town on the North Coast of California. While Rufus didn't believe for a moment that Sally would settle there long, he thought it worth the time and money to send a telegram to an old friend. The last he'd heard, the man was serving out there as a cook, but Zachary Taylor's response was of little help, as it read simply:

They are no longer here STOP Have no notion of where they are headed STOP

Taylor had always been a man given to compassion. Who knew where he currently placed his loyalties? That hadn't always been clear during the War Between the States, either.

Frustrated at being left to lick his wounds, he crumpled the message in his hand and pounded the desk with his closed fist. Forget those worthless miners. They'd never bring Sally back to him.

Jumping to his feet, he slammed his chair up against his deck. He then flattened out the telegram and proceeded to rip it into little pieces, scattering them across the floor. If Sally had left the lumber camp, it was obvious where she would eventually go – straight to Jack Harvey, should the man be stupid enough to open his arms to her.

Brushing his hands together, he left behind the shreds of his failed attempts at finding Sally and set about turning the tide of his war. Battles may be lost along the way, but the stronger man always gained the ultimate victory.

Sally was restless. If only she had enough money to take a stage or buy a horse — anything to avoid walking all the way to Oregon. At this rate, she and Jack would never get to see each other again.

She kept her face to the ground, watching as her new, sturdier shoes — finally broken in — made their way across the forest floor, through ferns and small bushes and sorrel.

Myghal bumped her shoulder with his. "There ain't nothin' new on the ground that we haven't been seein' for miles."

Looking up into Myghal's kind, laughing eyes, she couldn't help but smile. "You don't have to slow down on my behalf. You'd probably prefer Joe's company to mine."

She gazed at Joe's back. The man kept a steady pace way ahead of them, hardly taking any breaks each day and never letting Sally forget that it was her fault he had to leave his job in the lumber town. It didn't matter how many times she told him and Myghal that they didn't have to come with her because she was a grown woman who could find her own way to Oregon. Being the "gentlemen" that they were, they insisted on "escorting" her — more like a prisoner than a princess, to her way of thinking.

Myghal snorted. "Ye think I'd prefer the company of ol' Stonewall Jackson up there?"

Sally laughed, and the release of tension made her pack feel just a bit lighter. If it weren't for Myghal, she didn't think she could stand Joe's bitter silence.

"Have ye been to the ocean?"

"No," she replied, surprised at Myghal's unexpected question. "But we're not far from it, right?"

He flashed a secretive smile. "I'm thinkin' we should veer west and see it, then. But first, I heard from some folks in that town we stopped at last night that there's another sight we can't be missin'."

"And what sight would that be?" She let Myghal lead the way through the brush and between the trees as she waited for his response.

"It's a sight worth seein', and that's all ye'll be gettin' from me." His glance back at her said that he was loving the thought of surprising her. A small part of Sally's heart thawed with the pleasure of that realization.

"When will I get to see it?"

"Soon."

"And when will that be?"

"Are ya always this impatient, lass?"

"Hmmm…" She waited until she caught his eye, then with a broad smile she said, "Always."

He chuckled, and Sally was pleased.

After the sun was over halfway done with its trip across the sky, Joe finally stopped and allowed the group to rest and eat.

"We aren't in any hurry, Joe." Sally climbed onto a stump that must have been made when people were settling the nearby area and building their cabins. She relished the opportunity to look down on the boys, which didn't come often given her short stature. Popping the last bite of a biscuit in her mouth, she waited for Joe's inevitably negative response.

Joe tore at the grass near his boots. "*You* might not be in any hurry, but some of us have greater ambitions in life than just running away from all our problems."

Oh, yes. When it came to negativity and hurtful words, Joe never let her down.

"Come now, that's not fair." Myghal cradled his biscuit in his palm while raising an eyebrow at Joe. "What do you think ye were doin' when ya left Virginia City?"

Sally ran a hand through her blond waves, waiting. When Joe didn't offer a reply, she smirked, but one glance at Myghal's now-lowered brows and her gloating smile turned into a frown. Spinning around on the stump, she took in the view of tree-covered hills and tossed her hair in the boys' direction. *Men.* What did they really want from her, anyway?

"It's my turn to lead now." There was no question or malice in Myghal's voice. He sounded confident, hopeful even.

"Where are ya takin' us?" Joe growled, causing Sally to grin. Who was more like a dog now?

"You're as bad as Miss Sally. Would ya two just trust me fer once?"

There was no arguing with that. Turning, she found both Joe and Myghal watching her. Waiting.

She looked down at her dress and then back up at them. "What?"

Both quickly bent to gather up their things.

It was silly, really, but she couldn't keep the blush from heating her face. With a shake of her head, she jumped down from the stump, eager for their trio to be on its way again.

Over the course of the afternoon they turned inland, leaving the thick forest behind for grassy hillsides and blue skies. Sally felt excited and a bit nervous, wanting so very much to like Myghal's surprise. She trailed behind the men, partly because she had a hard time matching their pace, and partly because she was still avoiding Joe, just as she had been ever since they left Eureka. He'd been so generous, buying her two practical and modest traveling dresses, new shoes, and other supplies for their trip. He never demanded that Sally tell them why exactly she was so determined to get to Oregon, but the unspoken question hung between them ever since Joe and Myghal had found her that first night. He seemed determined to make sure she understood this "whim" of hers was costing him dearly.

As the sun began to set, they came upon Myghal's surprise so suddenly that Sally almost ran into Joe before she noticed they had stopped. Peeking around his broad back, she gasped.

"Oh..."

The gentle, green slopes were covered with purple flowers, all standing tall and bright in the last kiss of sunlight. They cascaded down the hill like a royal waterfall, swaying slightly in the evening breeze.

She let her pack and bedroll fall from her shoulders. "How beautiful!"

And it was – prettier than any of the flashy clothes Jacob had given her to attract men and more vibrant than anything she could remember seeing.

Without another thought, she started walking through the flowers. For a moment, she wished that no one else was there with her, just so she could run and dance through the carpet of color without anyone watching.

Eventually, she knelt down beside one of the flowers and examined it. Little round petals climbed up the stem, purple and white, glorious and pure. She placed her finger on one of the petals, fitting her fingertip to the gentle touch of the bloom. Her daddy had always told her that God would never leave her and never let go of her hand. Closing her eyes, she imagined God reaching out to her through the sweet caress of a flower.

"They're called lupines. Sure, an' they're a sight."

Reluctantly opening her eyes, she found Myghal standing close by, gazing out on the hillsides. She shook off her fancies. Her daddy hadn't known all the horrid things she'd do once she left home. He might have had other things to tell her about God's view of her if he had.

She stood and brushed her fingers across Myghal's sleeve. "This is a great surprise. It's beautiful."

He rolled his shoulder. "I thought ye might enjoy it." She was awarded with a small grin before he added, with a hint of melancholy, "Makes me miss my Irish mother, and our home in Cornwall."

"Oh?"

When he didn't respond, she whispered, "It makes me miss home, too."

Something stirred and then clenched painfully in his heart as Joe observed Myghal and Sally standing side by side in a pool of purple flowers. Her hair spread across her back and shoulders, standing out like gold against the plain brown dress he'd bought for her. A bit of wind picked up several pieces of her hair and set it to shimmering – like sunlight on clear water. Her stance suggested she was comfortable with Myghal, who was as tall and thin as Sally was small and curvy.

Huffing, Joe set his pack down next to theirs. Why was he even here, anyway? He kept waiting for Sally to tell them what her game was, but she continued to keep them in the dark, expecting them to take care of her. Spoiled, that's what the girl was.

He set out to talk with Sally, hoping to finally get the truth out of her. Myghal saw him coming and intercepted him before he could reach her. His grip on Joe's arm was firm, his voice quiet. "Not now, Joe. Let her enjoy the evenin'."

Joe scowled. "We've let her enjoy weeks without any questions. Don't ya think it's about time she tells us what her plan is?"

Something dangerous sparked in Myghal's normally calm gaze. "Not now."

Crossing his arms over his chest, Joe considered Myghal. The man was years older than him, probably already in his thirties, although his fun-loving ways often made him appear much younger. He hardly ever made demands, and Joe figured he owed him more respect than he often showed. With a brief nod, he acquiesced. "But we *will* ask her. Soon."

Myghal didn't reply but headed over to where they had left their belongings.

Glancing over at Sally, Joe found her sitting among the flowers again, looking past him to the sunset. With a sigh, he approached her, running a hand through his hair in frustration. "Mind if I join ya?"

She plucked a flower and fiddled with the stem. "Contrary to what you seem to think of me, I'm not the one giving the orders around here. So do what you want."

With a grumble, he plopped down next to her. After a moment, the calm of the setting sun and their surroundings made his shoulders drop a little lower and his breathing slow down a little more. The silence embraced them for a few moments, finally broken when Sally asked, "Do you have any regrets?"

"Yeah." Was there any other answer?

"Oh." She held the flower between her hands, quiet again.

His hand came up, and, after a brief hesitation, he tucked a strand of hair behind her ear. "What do you regret?" he asked in a deep whisper.

Picking a petal off the stem, she rubbed it between her fingers before holding it to her cheek. A lone tear fell onto the petal as she replied, "Falling in love."

He swallowed, unable to look away. "Was it really love?"

Her head came up, her watery gaze meeting his. "What?"

He wasn't sure how to respond. Clearing his throat, he

asked instead, "Who was he?"

She shook her head and got to her feet. "Forget I said anything."

"Sally…"

When she looked down at him, he held out the flower she had dropped in her haste. "Will you ever stop running? Myghal and I – how can we help you if you don't tell us what's goin' on?" He cringed, realizing he was heading into the territory forbidden by Myghal.

She grasped the flower, holding it close as she turned to see the last glimpse of sunset. "I don't know if anyone can help me anymore."

Chapter 10

TRUE TO HIS WORD, Myghal led them northwest, keeping them headed toward Oregon while still detouring to see the ocean. Sally had been landlocked since birth, although she had always longed to travel down the Mississippi River. To think – now she would get to see the Pacific Ocean!

The moment she glimpsed the place where the blue sky met the blue sea in an undefined horizon, she felt her heart soar. It was like Oregon, in a way, as it symbolized something beyond her present troubles. There was something infinitely hopeful in the constant motion of it, as well as the uncertainty of all it contained and where it might lead. She decided she loved the ocean, and felt an impulsive desire to live on the coast someday.

"'Tis another grand sight. I haven't seen it in a long time." Myghal gave a contented sigh.

Sally clasped her hands tightly together and held them against her chest in supplication. "Can we camp here tonight? Here on the beach?" *Oh, please!* It was hard to contain her childlike excitement at experiencing warm sand, powerful waves, and the crashing, promising noise of the surf.

Myghal snatched his hat from his head and nodded. "Sure. We'll build ourselves a grand ol' bonfire and let the sounds of the sea lull us to sleep."

With a sly grin, she replied, "Why, Myghal, you sound like a poet."

"I'm a musician, which isn't too far from a poet, ya know."

A frown stole away his good cheer. "Too bad I can't borrow meself a fiddle..."

The thought of lively music made Sally bounce on her toes. "I wish you could. But we mustn't let that ruin this perfect day."

"Perfect day, huh?" Joe looked skeptical while he took a wide stance on the sand, as if he feared he would sink or the waves would sneak up on him.

Sally motioned for Joe to follow and performed a little twirl. "Come on. Take off your boots and we'll go splash in the water. Unless you're afraid...?"

She hoped to badger his pride until he agreed, but he stood his ground.

"I'm not eager to get wet or carried out to sea, if it's all the same to you."

She grabbed his sleeve, trying to tug him along. "Can't you just have some fun? You've never seen anything like this in dry, dirty ol' Virginia City."

"Thank heavens," he mumbled just loud enough for her to hear. "Look, Sally, you may not have liked Virginia City all that much, but to me, it's home. I much prefer such a place to the thought of drowning."

He looked genuinely uncomfortable, so she finally gave up and left him behind, pulling off her new shoes and running with bare feet through the glorious, non-desert sand. But when she ran straight into the waves, she gasped at the fearful rush of cold that knocked her over.

"Careful, lass!" Myghal helped her up, his own bare feet leaving prints in the dark, wet sand.

"It's freezing! I thought... I hoped....maybe..."

"Ye thought it would be warm? Surprised, were ya?"

"A bit."

A hidden laugh gleamed in Myghal's eyes as the icy water

swirled around their legs. Wanting to surprise him as much as he kept surprising her, she waited until the water started to pull at them before pushing him into the retreating wave. As he stumbled to his knees, she giggled, then ran away along the beach.

She hadn't gone far before a thin but strong arm caught her around the waist and lifted her, laughing and screaming, into the air. Another wave took them both down, but Myghal kept a firm grip on her as the water surrounded them, then left them in soggy silence.

Coughing some of the gritty sand and salt water from her mouth, she felt Myghal remove his arm while placing his other hand on her shoulder. "Are ya all right?"

"I haven't laughed like that since I left home." Catching a glimpse of Myghal's short red hair sticking up at various angles, she giggled again. "You're a sight, Myghal."

He smiled, but didn't laugh as he replied, "So are you."

His heart pounded with an intensity that scared him as Joe watched Myghal and Sally fall backward into the ocean. The sensible part of his mind told him that they were only playing, that Myghal would make sure Sally was safe. But the other, irrational part of his mind urged him to protect Sally himself.

He was just about ready to get up and drag Sally from the dangerous grip of the sea – and, if he were honest, from the grip of his friend – when he saw her and Myghal finally get up and head over to where he had started a fire using driftwood. Scavenging through his bag, he came up with a blanket, which he handed to Sally as she sat down next to him.

Unsure what to do about the roiling emotions that were leaving him seasick, he poked at the fire and kept trying to shoot a glare at Myghal, who wasn't meeting his gaze. Frustrated, he decided it was finally time to get some truth out of Sally.

"So, what are we really getting ourselves into by taking you to Oregon?"

"What do you mean?"

Sally wasn't meeting his gaze either, which infuriated him even more. He picked up a piece of driftwood from a pile he'd stacked earlier and rubbed it between his hands. "I mean, why are you goin' to Oregon? Why are you dragging us…?"

She jerked her head up, the fire reflected in her eyes. "I'm not dragging you anywhere. You insisted on following me."

"To make sure you were safe."

"I'm never safe! Don't ya understand? When I decided to leave home, I left everything that was safe and good and right."

The fire popped in reply, crackling steadily, hungrily. He fed it with the piece of driftwood he had been gripping and watched Myghal throw in a few pieces, as well.

"I don't understand, Sally. Help me understand."

He didn't really expect a response anymore, but that didn't stop him from letting her know that he really did want her to explain herself. As he watched her intently, he saw her shoulders drop and the reluctance slowly melt away. "His name was Jack."

Joe saw Myghal's head come up out of the corner of his eye, but he continued to stare at Sally, afraid she would suddenly close up again.

"I loved him. And he made me believe he loved me, too. He always talked about the places we would go and the things we would see.

"But then one day he said he hated to leave me, but he had to go to Virginia City – to try to find another silver vein or some such nonsense. He had talked about nothing else for months, so I knew his heart was set on it. Of course, my parents refused to let me go with him. They said a mining town was no place for their daughter. And they were right."

She didn't take her eyes off of the fire, and her face reddened with the heat and anger and pain.

"Jack and I were meant to be together. I had known that for years. So without telling anyone, including Jack, I took the same train as him, hoping to surprise him when we got to Virginia City. I definitely surprised him." Her voice was hard, bitter. "He told me to go home. Said I didn't belong there. I begged and begged, but he left me standing in the middle of the street with no money and nowhere to go. I would have starved if it wasn't for Jacob and his brothel."

A simmering rage raced through Joe's blood, making him desperate to find this Jack and beat him senseless for leaving an idealistic, hopeful girl alone in such a place, without any means of caring for herself other than selling her body. How innocent and trusting had Sally once been to end up in such a situation?

"Sally, I…"

"I'm going to find him."

Taken aback, Joe hesitated. "Find who?"

"Jack. He lives in Oregon now. I found out from a miner who used to know him."

"You're goin' to find Jack?"

"Yes. And he'll pay for what he's done – either by taking me in as he ought to have done three years ago, or by…by…some other way. I'll think of something."

She had taken that coin pouch from the front of her dress and fiddled with it, eyes closed as the light of the flames danced across her face.

Joe was stunned into silence. He certainly had a similar desire to find Jack and make him pay, but it bothered him to think of Sally seeking revenge. Why, she had left the security of a good job as a cook's helper in a lumber town – made them all leave their jobs – to take them on some crazy quest to chase down a man who obviously didn't care a whit about her.

Across from them, Myghal sat with his head in his hands. Wasn't he going to say something about this crazy revelation?

Joe cleared his throat. "So we're escorting you to the man who left you as a prostitute rather than marry you? Is that what yer tellin' us?"

Her eyes fairly blazed with fury as she glared at him. "This isn't about you. Either of you."

"Oh, it isn't, is it? Well, whether you like it or not, you've dragged us into this sorry mess."

"Then why don't ya just leave? A girl who's survived as a prostitute for three years certainly doesn't need anyone to come and rescue her now. It's too late. It's too late..."

She turned and stormed away, and all that was left were her sobs, the crackle of the fire, and the roar of the sea.

Chapter 11

FOG SHROUDED THE BEACH and what was left of Sally's broken heart. She didn't want to wake up – didn't want to face another day traveling with Joe and Myghal. How could she expect them to understand? She simply had to find Jack.

That thought followed her throughout the morning as they ate a simple breakfast of cold, leftover flapjacks and jerky, then packed up their few belongings and headed out, ever inland and northward bound.

Sally didn't bother trying to keep up with Joe's faster pace. Instead, she fell farther and farther behind. Myghal took the middle position, staying behind Joe but turning around every so often to make sure she hadn't disappeared. As stubborn as these two men were, there was no hope of escaping them again, but she could at least show defiance in her own way.

It was almost evening by the time Joe decided they could stop. Sally's feet were in agony, but she kept her mouth shut, determined to hold onto what little independence she could still claim. Myghal and Joe seemed to be determined, as well – determined to keep their distance, which was more than fine. At least that's what she whispered to her throbbing heart that matched the beat of her throbbing feet.

After they ate a small supper, Myghal went straight to sleep, while Joe kept the first watch of the night as he leaned up against a tree. Not a word had been spoken between any of them except, "Pass the biscuits."

Suddenly, Sally was starved for communication. She didn't

want to face her nightmares quite yet, and it was too painful to lie awake in silence. So she climbed out of her bedroll and walked over to Joe, sitting down beside him and hoping that he wouldn't send her away.

He didn't.

"What do ya want, Sally?"

"Whatever happened between you and Elizabeth?"

She'd heard bits and pieces – gossip that had filtered down from the rest of Jacob's girls and some nosy miners who loved nothing better than a good heartbreak story. But she wanted to hear Joe's side from his own mouth.

"She never loved me." He stared unblinkingly at the fire a few feet away.

"But you were going to be married, weren't you? She must have loved you."

He shook his head. "She loved David."

A fire rose in Sally's face at the mention of the man's name. David was the one who came to Jacob that night, wanting answers about why the brothel owner was deceiving Elizabeth, Jacob's sister. At least, those were the words he spoke aloud. But Sally knew betrayal and hurt when she saw it. The man was upset about something that had just happened, and if Sally was any good at reading body language, she knew that "something" had to do with his girl and another man. She recognized the agony written on his face as the same stabbing sensation she had felt when Jack left. Seeing David like that, she suddenly hadn't felt alone.

I know what it's like to be cast aside. But we can make each other feel wanted tonight.

She had never made such an offer before. Always, it was Jacob setting up her nights or another man approaching her as she danced or played cards with the whole sorry lot of them. But that one time she made the proposition. She wanted to heal this man's heart, and maybe, in the process, he would heal hers.

They had only been in each other's arms for a moment, just started kissing and letting go of their cares, when Myghal dumped the contents of her room's water pitcher over them. Myghal was David's friend, and as such he was protecting the man – from her. He led David away, leaving Sally alone once again. She saw no one else that night as she sobbed into her pillow, feeling for all the world like Jack had left her again.

Remembering all that had transpired, she realized that Joe was the man who had caused David all that misery. It was Joe who had fallen in love with David's girl.

Inexplicable anger filled her. "So she loved David, huh? And knowing that, you still tried to steal her away from him." Bitterness punctuated her words as they hung in the smoky air.

Joe finally looked at her, his fists clenched tight. "It wasn't like I chose to love her despite David's feelings. It just happened. Love isn't a choice."

"Isn't it?" She didn't really know what she was asking. It didn't feel like a choice when it came to her feelings for Jack. So why was she goading Joe?

"You tell me. And when you find out all the secrets of love and the answer to a perfect relationship, come back and let me know." He spat the words at her, his sandy hair falling across his forehead like a cloud crossing the moon. Mysterious. Frightening.

Reaching out, she brushed his hair back, not wanting his eyes to be shadowed. She needed to see his emotions, wanted to know what he was thinking.

He captured her wrist, and her hand moved down to his bristly cheek, cupping his face. There was nothing more to say, for he knew as well as she that she had no such answers, but seeing the vulnerability in his amber eyes, she suddenly wished she could put his heart – and her own – at ease.

Her eyes drifted to his mouth. A kiss in this moment would be explosive and far too difficult to contain. So, while all of her training and experiences over the past three years begged her to linger, she drew back and slowly slid her fingers down and away from his face.

"Good night, Joe," she murmured, turning away from him and the fire.

Sally's touch lingered for weeks, just as the words from their conversation echoed in his head. Joe wanted to throw the girl over his shoulder and haul her back to Falk – or maybe even to Virginia City, to his brother's ranch. Ranching suited him, so maybe it was time to face the past as Sally was doing and find the life he once loved, despite the fact that he didn't approve of her head-on manner. What on God's green earth could she hope to gain by searching for Jack again? The man obviously never wanted to be found.

Before any of them seemed prepared for it, they arrived at the Deschutes River – at the spot in central Oregon where Jack was supposed to have settled. The river was bright and wide and wild. The land around it held a certain vast solitude that reminded him of Nevada, although the terrain here was different. Volcanic rocks formed craggy peaks across the landscape, and the place seemed somehow more alive and hopeful than Virginia City. Joe had to admit that the area was beautiful.

The least prepared of them, perhaps, was Sally herself, as far as Joe could tell. She had been quieter since their detour to see the ocean, but now she was stone silent. The first time they caught sight of what appeared to be Jack's cabin in the distance, Sally's face drained of color.

He put his arm around her to steady her – and himself.

"Are ya sure you want to do this?"

Why couldn't she just forget the whole ridiculous thing? It was unrealistic to expect anything but disdain from this man, but more than that, Joe feared that her apparent desire might be fulfilled. What if Sally and Jack shared the same sort of connection that Elizabeth and David did? David had left Elizabeth, too, but she still chose him over Joe. His heart couldn't take such an emotional beating again.

"Of course I want to do this."

She lifted her chin, but her voice lacked any conviction. She leaned heavily against him, and he turned, grabbing her upper arms and trying to catch her gaze.

"Sally? Look at me."

She did, right before she fainted.

Gathering her into his arms, he looked helplessly to Myghal. "She can't be serious about doing this. I don't know why we even allowed this to come as far as it has. We should just go."

Myghal worked his jaw, looking like he wanted to agree with Joe. Instead, he replied, "Ye know we cain't. She'll never forgive us if we don't let her say what she came here to say."

"Ya think she only wants to say something?" He pulled her tighter against his chest, weighing his options and Sally's possible courses of action. "You know Sally. She's not goin' to settle for mere words. The man will either take her back or face some sort of outrageous plan of revenge."

"I know."

"I don't want either of those things to happen." He glanced down at her pale face, wishing he had some sort of control over her, wishing she would listen.

"Neither do I."

"So what are we goin' to do?"

Sighing and rubbing his hands on his ragged pants,

Myghal said, "We're just goin' to be right here. We both know this isn't goin' to end well fer her, but she's got to see that for herself – we'll never convince her of it. So we'll just be there fer her when that good-for-nothin' man breaks her heart again."

Joe lifted his gaze to the winding river and the distant mountains. *I want to do more.*

He couldn't say the words out loud, because he knew that what Myghal said was true. Sally was determined to face Jack, to have her love reciprocated or avenged.

Sally stirred in his arms, and, in that moment before she gained consciousness, he drew her close and leaned his forehead down to touch hers. Then he kissed her cheek, a light brush like the breeze on the river. He decided then and there that he would be there for her, no matter what happened.

When she opened her eyes, he mustered a smile. "Are ya all right?"

"Did I faint?" She sounded confused, lost.

"Yeah."

She sighed, her lashes settling like feathers against her soft skin. "I'm sorry." She didn't try to explain it away. There was no need.

Slowly, he set her down, keeping an arm around her waist to make sure she could stand without his help. She looked out at Jack's cabin again, hesitantly taking a step forward, away from him. He longed to hold her again, to bring her back. But he let her go.

After a few steps, she looked back at him and Myghal. "You – you won't leave without me?" There was a note of pleading in her voice.

"No, Sally. We'll be right here. Unless you want me to come...?"

She shook her head. "No. I'll be fine. I just wanted to be sure..."

He nodded, understanding her fear and wanting to go with her just so he could make Jack regret his part in causing it.

Then she turned her back on both of them and headed straight to Jack's front door. She looked so small against the winding length of the river that was shining painfully bright in the afternoon sunshine.

Joe shielded his eyes with one hand and clenched his other hand into a fist. No matter what the outcome, he knew that this moment would haunt him for years to come.

Chapter 12

THREE YEARS. An eternity. A moment in time. And now she was walking up to Jack's front porch as if she were coming to greet a new neighbor. Her head hurt, her stomach fluttered, and tears sprang to her eyes. All this time, and she had never decided what exactly she would say when she saw him again. A thousand words had been spoken to her reflection in the mirror behind Jacob's bar, but now not one came to mind. All she wanted to do was fling herself into his arms as soon as he opened the door.

With all the seriousness and expectation of a walk down a church aisle, she made her way up the porch steps, but she couldn't bring herself to knock on the door. She stood frozen, feeling as scared as she had the day Jack left. What if he abandoned her again? Surely her heart would be crushed beyond repair.

A sudden movement brought her wide eyes to the window. As if she were seeing her dreams playing out before her startled gaze, she saw Jack – sporting a dark, well-trimmed beard and a look of contentment she had never seen before – sitting at a crude little table. Oh, he looked better than he ever had before! He was a mature man, settled down just as she had always wished.

Then something else in the room moved. A woman approached the table, a bright smile on her face and wisps of brown hair covering her smooth forehead. She seemed...happy. Brushing some flour off of her apron, the woman leaned close to Jack and kissed him. When they pulled back, their eyes met for a long moment, and they shared a smile – so similar to the ones Jack had given Sally, but this one wasn't for her.

Biting her lip, Sally put her hand to the glass. Never had she expected this. Jack had found someone else, and he was happy.

After a brief moment, the cold of the window glass seeped into her hand, and she gasped, bringing a hand to her mouth. *He's happy.* Her heart thrilled to see it just a second before it plummeted, leaving her sick and weary.

Irrationally, she longed to meet Jack's gaze, to know that what they'd shared was real – that he hadn't forgotten. But the pain in her chest told her it was real for her, no matter what Jack had felt.

Keeping her trembling fingers to her lips, she turned and fled. Off the porch. Away from where she had left Joe and Myghal. Anywhere. Away.

Landing somewhere by the edge of the river, she waited for the tears to come. Her hand hovered over the clear water, a mere pulse of her heart away from touching the window glass again. Her breath came in short, ragged gasps. But no tears came.

Plunging her hand into the river, she brought it back out with a cry and a splash of frigid water to her dry cheeks.

Something was over, and a part of her wouldn't accept it. While her brain had been preoccupied with daily survival, her heart had repeated Jack's name so many times that she had eventually defined her future happiness with that one word – *Jack*. Marrying Jack. Loving Jack. Growing old with Jack. Laughing with Jack. Basking in Jack's smile. Hiding in Jack's arms.

Now someone else had claimed that happiness. And where did that leave her?

Looking up at the cruel, sunny sky, she whispered, "God, I... I don't know... I can't..."

A gentle hand touched her shoulder, and finally the tears fell. First, one slid down her cheek, then another, and then she began to sob. Heaving, she leaned over the river.

Water to water. Ashes to ashes. Dust to dust.

A mirror mocking her, telling her that all her rehearsals behind the bar never changed anything.

Broken glass cutting up her heart – bleeding, bleeding, bleeding...

Sally's nightmares had become reality, and Joe couldn't fix the problem by waking her up. He wished he could, because her gut-wrenching, hopeless sobs were breaking his heart.

All he could do was sit there beside her, reminding her that she wasn't alone. He kept his hand on her shoulder – a physical connection that spoke of a promise to stay by her side.

She was crying so hard that Joe began to worry she would make herself really ill. "Sally..."

He couldn't tell her it would be all right. He couldn't say anything that would comfort her. So he pulled her into his embrace and held her close, not speaking a word.

As Sally gripped his shirt, Joe looked up and saw Myghal standing nearby, several yards from the riverbank. Joe had never seen the man look so distraught. His hands shook before forming into fists, and his eyes locked on Sally with a deep, commiserating sorrow, but he didn't come any closer.

Resting his cheek on her soft hair, Joe prayed silently for mercy.

Part II:

Fear Not

"Thou drewest near in the day that I called upon thee: thou saidst, Fear not."

Lamentations 3:57

Chapter 13

IS THIS HOW A GIRL *is supposed to feel on her wedding day?*

Sally glanced down at her plain, white cotton dress, smoothing the skirt with trembling fingers. The trip back to California had been solemn, as if accompanied by the sounds of a funeral march. In a way, it had been. Her cries had filled her sleepless nights as she mourned the death of a love that never should have died.

Somehow, they made it back to these hills fifty miles north of Eureka, where the lupines had enchanted them weeks ago. Most of the flowers were dried up now, but the grass was still green, and Joe agreed they wouldn't find a better place to get married.

She sat down in the grass, tired of waiting for Joe to finish talking with the preacher they had brought back with them from the closest town. She couldn't fathom what the man must think of them and of her, especially, and her insistence that their wedding take place outdoors and not in a church. It was the only issue she had voiced on the subject, too weary to fight on Joe's behalf.

He deserved someone better, someone desirable, but she didn't have the heart to push her only hope away. Who else would ever marry her? Perhaps Rufus might still have her, but he wasn't an option.

And Jack would never be hers again.

Sensing someone watching her, she looked up to find Myghal standing a few feet away, holding something in his hands. He approached and sat down beside her, one knee bent close to his chest, the other stretched out before him. A moment passed before he set the flowering stems on her skirt.

"I found these growin' at the edge o' the woods. A woman should have flowers on her wedding day."

The blushing pink of the flowers stood out against the white of her dress. Her breath caught in her throat as she studied them. The puffy little blooms resembled hearts dripping blood, or perhaps tears.

Her gaze flew to Myghal's face, but he wasn't looking at her. He was playing with a blade of grass, staring at the fog drifting over the distant hills.

She didn't know what to say, or what to make of his offering. Reaching out to touch one of the blossoms, her hand shook, and she thought better of it, afraid to crush the beautiful, fragile gift. She clutched her hands together and set them in her lap, a safe distance away from the flowers.

"I won't be goin' back to Virginia City with ye. I thought I'd give Falk another chance."

She nodded, unable to respond.

He flexed his fingers, his arm resting across his knee and his hand dangling in the space between them. "Joe's a good man. He'll take care of ya, but ye will have to be patient with him."

The idea of Myghal taking Joe's place briefly floated through her mind like a cloud crossing the murky gray of the sky. As soon as it appeared, it blended into the background of her thoughts. It was a wisp that couldn't be contained. Myghal was an adventurer who wouldn't settle down – not for the likes of her, anyway.

She tossed her head, trying to jar her mind's wicked wanderings, ashamed. Joe was a good man, and she should be grateful he was willing to take her, to provide for her. She only wished she could wear the dress he bought her with no guilt, and no memories of past indiscretions and heartbreak staining its purity.

"Myghal, I…"

No longer hearing the rumble of Joe's voice mixed with the gravel of the reverend's, she glanced back. They were heading their direction. Both determination and a sense of pleading for something she couldn't define churned in her stomach.

"It'll be all right, lass."

Myghal's hand hovered in her vision, and she looked up and finally met his gaze, her heart in her eyes. His soft smile gave her the strength to meet Joe with a small smile of her own.

There was once a time, not so very long ago, when Joe would have been too afraid to ask someone to marry him…again. That was before he had gotten to know someone with a genuinely broken and bleeding heart like his – someone who needed him. Together, they could help each other heal. He had promised, if only to himself, that he would be there for her. And so he would.

With Sally by his side as his wife he returned to Virginia City. Neither of them preferred the place with its terrible memories, but it was home for him. Running the ranch with his brother was what he had been raised to do, and he was done running away. Judging by his wife's quiet compliance, he guessed she was done running, too.

When their train arrived in Virginia City, Sally shivered next to him on the seat. He wrapped his arm around her shoulders and held her close. Rubbing her arm to comfort her and still her quaking, he was transported back to the day he and Myghal found her in the woods outside of Eureka – utter exhaustion evident in her countenance. She seemed exhausted now, too, but in a different sort of way. He wished there was some way he could revive her.

"We're here."

She shivered again when he whispered the words into her ear. Dare he hope it was from pleasure?

He gathered up their few belongings and then tucked her arm into his, escorting her off of the train and into the blinding autumn sunlight. Tugging his hat brim lower to shade his eyes, he glanced around before leading Sally up the steps and onto the street. He skimmed the passersby for a glimpse of his brother, but he was nowhere to be seen.

"The town is dying."

Looking down in surprise at Sally, Joe waited for her to clarify, but she didn't say anything else, and she didn't meet his questioning gaze.

He stared up the hill. People still swarmed the streets, but more like a group of flies buzzing over a dead carcass than the pack of wolves that used to roam the town. The pounding of mining machinery sounded more like gasps for breath than the heavy, incessant heartbeat it used to be. If he hadn't grown up with the town, he might not have been able to pinpoint the subtle differences, but they were there. Miners had already started to move on years ago, and the town had nothing left to offer but the lives and businesses that had been planted too deeply to be uprooted.

He finally replied, "I reckon yer right." It ate at him to dwell on it, though, so he nudged her shoulder, pointed to the livery, and said, "Come on."

If his brother wasn't going to be kind enough to meet him here, he would have to find some other transportation down into the canyon.

Unlike Elizabeth, Sally had never been to the Clifton ranch. It bothered her that she should think of another woman right now, but she couldn't help but consider the fact that Joe never would have imagined bringing a prostitute home as his wife. He had dreamed of a decent girl who was all sweetness and innocence – something Sally could never be again.

Reining in the horses they had rented from the livery, they stopped in front of the ranch house, neither one saying a word. For a moment, Sally hoped that Joe would carry her over the threshold, like a real lady.

But Seth Clifton appeared in the doorway, barring the path to her daydreams. His clothes were rumpled, his eyes bloodshot, and his stance unsteady.

He's drunk…or was not that long ago.

Joe swung off of his horse and ran up to his brother, grasping Seth's upper arms. "What's happened? You look awful!"

Seth stared beyond him and met Sally's uncertain gaze. "That your wife?" He gestured to where she sat, still atop her horse. The whole situation didn't feel right, and Sally clutched the saddle horn tighter.

Joe ignored his brother's question. "What happened, Seth?"

He's ashamed of me.

"She died."

"Who died?" Realization washed over his face a moment later. "Naomi? Naomi died?"

Seth pushed past Joe, staggered down the porch steps, and approached Sally. Letting go of the saddle horn, she gripped the reins and clamped her jaw shut to still the tremors and the bitter words aching to leave her mouth. Seth's hair and eyes were darker than Joe's, but the somber demeanor was the same, and she couldn't help but wonder…

Is this how Joe will be as a husband?

Joe followed after his brother, rubbing his moustache with finger and thumb in agitation. His uncertainty and his mussed-up, sandy hair made him look like a little boy.

Grabbing the reins from Sally's hands, most likely to steady himself, Seth scrutinized her. She knew her gaze was hard, untrusting, but she didn't know how to change her wary habits. They had served her well the past three years.

"She ain't Elizabeth," Seth finally said.

Joe growled a warning to his brother, although his lack of action suggested he was still in shock.

"No, I ain't," she mimicked.

"That's too bad." Seth backed up then and returned to the house, slamming the front door shut after he entered. Sally stared after him, wondering how much of his disapproval came from grief. A soft touch on her leg startled her and brought her gaze down to Joe.

"I'm sorry, Sally. I didn't know... My brother isn't normally this way. I just cain't believe..."

"I know." She allowed Joe to put his hands on her waist and help her down from the horse, but as soon as her feet touched the ground she stepped away from him. If she were Elizabeth, she might have expected to be carried over the threshold and to receive a warm welcome.

But she wasn't Elizabeth.

It was settled. Myghal had made a commitment to be there for Sally, but such a commitment had to be broken when she agreed to marry someone other than him.

Ah, but it isn't the first time I've lost a lass to someone else, is it?

He gave himself a shake. There was no purpose in reminding himself of such things. He didn't have the energy to survive in a swamp of regrets.

"Here again, are ya?"

Myghal looked up from his spot by the doorway to see Mr. Taylor clearing the dirty dishes from the long wooden table in the cookhouse. He had purposely come to visit when none of the other loggers remained. Since it was a Saturday evening, most of them were gathering in the dance hall.

"Yes, I am." He picked up a plate and followed Taylor into the kitchen.

"Never thought I'd see you and your friends again. How long have you been back?"

Myghal set the dish down next to the washbasin. "A couple o' weeks. Thought it was time to catch up with ye."

"Is Sally with you, then?"

"No." No matter how much he selfishly wished she was here with him, that would never change.

He shook his head, trying to free the stubborn, sappy thoughts that lingered in his mind. Sally didn't belong with him. Apparently, no woman did. It was just him and his fiddle and a handful of broken-hearted tunes. He wouldn't be able to play them if he was happily settled-down, now would he?

"What happened to her?"

The interest in Taylor's voice made Myghal feel suddenly defensive. "Why do ye ask?"

"I wouldn't be a friend if I didn't ask after her welfare."

Myghal folded his arms over his chest as he leaned against some cupboards. "A friend, is it?"

Taylor looked up from where he had started rinsing dishes. Studying Myghal for a moment, he finally added, "I was worried about her, is all. An old acquaintance of mine was asking after the three of ya…"

Myghal stood up straighter. "Who?"

"A man by the name of Rufus O'Daniel. He telegraphed me a while back wanting to know where you three were. I told him you had left and I had no idea where you had gone."

Myghal's heart began to pound painfully. Everyone in Virginia City knew of Rufus O'Daniel, and from what little he had heard, having the likes of him stalking after a gal was never a good sign. "And how do ye be knowin' Mr. O'Daniel?"

Taylor sighed but didn't turn around. "We both fought with the Confederates during the War Between the States. The point is that I know Rufus, and he's never been a gentleman when it comes to the ladies. I didn't like the thought of him having anything to do with Sally."

"Did ya hear from him again?"

"No. Nor do I want to. If you didn't come across him by now, I doubt you have anything to worry about."

"Hardly," Myghal mumbled as he made his way out of the kitchen.

"Where are ya goin' now?" Taylor called after him.

"To Nevada."

He strode to one of the tables and laid his palms on the surface, hanging his head. The tremors started in his arms and then began to rattle his insides, until he couldn't separate his heart and his mind, but that was nothing new for him.

Taylor gathered a few more dishes from the table. "You know that if you leave this job again, you'll likely never get it back."

"I know."

Myghal turned his head enough to see Taylor nod – perhaps in acquiescence, or approval, or farewell. When the kitchen door swung shut behind the man, Myghal pounded his fists against the table. If he were looking out for only his own interests, he wouldn't leave this place. In fact, the farther he was from Sally, the better. But Joe and Sally were his friends, no matter what the two of them now meant to each other.

Glancing down at his tightly clenched fists, he whispered,

"God, I don't know what Ye're doin', but, well, Ye've got a better view than I do, so I guess I'll let Ya lead the way. Just, please…"

He couldn't finish the thought. Thankfully, God could figure out his unspoken plea.

As he left the cookhouse, the damp chill took him back to Cornwall. *How many times can a man's heart break before it becomes beyond healin'?*

Chapter 14

THE BLUE SKY arced over the canyon, vivid and bright with un-shed tears. Between the dry and rocky walls, sagebrush, horses, the ranch buildings, and some tents dotted the landscape – not close enough together to ease the lonely atmosphere. Looking down at the small, sad grave, Sally wondered if this would be where she ended up, as well.

She was just as much an outcast from the so-called "polite" society of Virginia City as Seth's wife had been – if not more so. As a Jewish woman, Naomi had to be buried here in the canyon, in a Jewish cemetery that sat forlornly on a piece of the Clifton property. As a former prostitute, Sally had perhaps even less of a right to be buried in the grandiose cemetery in town that be-longed only to the good Catholics and those accepted by them.

A shiver racked her body as a sharp wind swept through the canyon. Sally pulled her shawl more tightly about her shoulders, longing to leave the wretched scene but held in place by the rhythmic beating of desert sand and dirt being flung onto a pathetic casket. Joe and Seth took turns filling up the hole in the ground, neither man saying a word. What could any of them say? Seth's wife had died of consumption mere days before his brother brought his new bride to the ranch.

Sally shifted her gaze away from the flying dirt that seemed to take the place of any falling tears, choosing to look instead upon the small headstone Seth had commissioned.

Naomi Clifton
Beloved Wife
1852-1886

Nothing else. No fancy poem. No words from Scripture. No intricate scrolling or other embellishments. And the size was a pebble in comparison to the ridiculous boulders up above in the main cemetery in Virginia City.

Crouching down beside it, Sally traced the words and numbers with her finger. The stone was so cold.

Closing her eyes, she pictured her own name on a headstone.

Sally Clay Clifton

Would it say "beloved wife"? Would Joe cry when the dirt rained down on her casket? Would anyone care that she was gone?

Sally didn't know if the tear that fell from her eye onto the headstone was for Naomi's death, Seth's loss, or her own uncertainty.

A shadow covered her, and she turned around to find Joe standing behind her, his shirt soaked with sweat and his face damp – with more sweat or with tears, she couldn't tell. Her heart constricted, and she slowly got to her feet.

A movement caught her eye, and she noted that Seth was walking back to the house. Seth was sullen in his grief, but when faced with the choice between his company and Joe's, her feet inched away from the man who claimed her as a wife but neglected to treat her as such.

She hadn't known how to act around him since their wedding day. Everything was different. She was beholden to him, dependent on him, but she couldn't figure out how he wanted her to repay him. Her teeth clenched and her fingers twitched as she continued to back away, hating that he wouldn't tell her what he expected of her, hating that they couldn't communicate. Despising the fact that they were committed to each other when they were so obviously ill-suited. What had they been thinking?

"Sally." She heard him say her name as she turned her back to him and ran the rest of the way to the house. He didn't follow her, and she moaned as she closed the front door because she wished he had.

Seth sat at the kitchen table, his head buried in his arms, not glancing up once at the sound of her approach despite the slamming of the door and the creaking of the floorboards. He looked as desperately lonely as she felt. She watched his back rise and fall for a minute, then roused herself and went to set a kettle on the stove.

After fixing some coffee, she poured and turned around to find Seth standing behind her. She gasped and put a hand to her heart, sloshing some of the hot liquid over the side of the tin cup.

"I'm sorry. I didn't mean to startle you." He reached for a cloth behind her and traded it for her cup. "I just wanted to see what you were doing."

It was the most he had said to her since she arrived, and the words were much gentler than his welcome had been. Wiping her hands, she gestured to the cup he held. "I was just making some coffee for you. You looked like you could use some."

He nodded, his gaze bouncing around the kitchen and landing everywhere but on her. "Do you cook?" he finally asked.

She wadded up the cloth. "Yes."

He nodded again. "I..." His gaze finally landed on her, serious and almost...hopeful. "I can help if you need anything."

The cloth fell from her hands. That was the last thing she

had expected him to say.

He set his cup on the table and bent down to pick up the cloth while she stood gaping at him. When he straightened, she took the cloth from him and stole a glimpse of Joe outside the window. She could just make out his stoic form across the canyon, still standing by the grave. Blinking from the brightness of the sunlight, she tore her gaze away in time to see Seth departing down the hall toward his room.

"Wait!"

He paused before opening his bedroom door.

"I wanted to make some fresh bread to go with our supper." She didn't know how to voice her request. After a moment of silence, she was ready to wave him back to his room, feeling ridiculous. She didn't need a man's help in the kitchen.

But he came back and said, "I'll show you where we keep everything."

She followed him around as he poked through cupboards, her breathing evening out and her shoulders relaxing.

Joe had no words for his brother. What sort of cruel irony was this – that he was newly married and his brother was in mourning? The night air whipped around him as he kept lonely vigil by the fresh grave. This was Seth's place, he knew, but Seth came no farther than the porch after the headstone had been placed. He just sat there in his rickety old chair with the orange glow of the end of his cigar as the only light.

Lifting clumps of sandy dirt before his face, Joe was tempted to rub them into his skin. He could never do anything right, it would seem. So why shouldn't he mourn properly, pouring "ashes" on his head? Naomi was a good, kind woman – much quieter than Sally, although Sally's cooking was more to his liking...

What sort of thought is that?

He brushed it away, along with the dirt clinging to his fingers. Some of the granules blew back onto his clothing, as if they knew he didn't deserve to be clean – or blessed. Elizabeth had been smart not to accept him and all his self-centered ways.

Now Sally was stuck with him, and he with her. They weren't a good fit. How could they be? A sassy, needy spoiled dove and a selfish, good-for-nothing raven that brought only death and bad tidings?

Turning away from the grave, he stalked through the chill, past the tiny orange glare of his brother's cigar, and into the house.

Sally sat on a chair by the window, the smell of fresh-baked bread surrounding her and making his stomach grumble, but not quite enticing enough to reach beyond the sick feeling he'd had ever since he'd heard of Naomi's death. He hadn't been able to think of eating anything all day.

Seeing Sally's position, Joe thought perhaps she had been watching him, although it seemed unlikely she could have seen anything in the darkness.

"Why don't ya have a lamp lit?"

"I don't know," she whispered, not glancing in his direction.

He sensed that this was a moment when he could do the right thing. He could light a lamp for her, offer her a comforting embrace, and tell her that life would settle down. It would all be fine soon.

But he couldn't seem to find the energy to be kind to her. Instead, he went into his bedroom and closed the door behind him.

One morning a couple of weeks after their arrival, Sally set extra bacon in a pan, relishing in the sizzling sound the pieces made as they cooked. Seth made the coffee and set out their cups just as Joe entered the room. He never said anything about Seth helping her out now and again, and she wished he would. In fact, she wished he would help her himself. If they could do something together – anything – maybe they could ease through the tension that settled over the house like fog.

She put two extra pieces of the crisp bacon on Joe's plate when it was ready, adding eggs and a buttered slice of bread. Joe nodded but didn't say a word the whole meal.

Neither Joe nor Seth thanked her before they went out to check on the horses. As she washed the dishes she compared their responses to those of other men she had been around in recent years. They had wanted her, always noticed her. There were ridiculous, flattering words and big, goofy smiles. Not genuine, really, but for a moment she longed for them. What good was it to be married to a man if he treated her like his burden to bear? Was this any better than if Jack had accepted her because she begged him to?

She sighed. After the incident with Jack, she had accepted Joe's proposal. He offered to protect her – to give her a place to stay, and a place for her heart to be hidden away from life's cruelties. She hadn't realized that releasing certain insecurities would only make room for insecurities of a different kind. Was it too much to ask for someone decent to truly love her? Considering the past few years, perhaps it was.

"I just need some attention again," she said aloud. It sounded dangerous even without anyone in the room to tell her so, but she ignored that thought. What harm could it be to just do some shopping and such in Virginia City?

Trying to find some pieces of confidence to sew back to-gether, she put the last dish back in the cupboard and headed out to the barn.

"Joe?" she called out to the stalls.

A head poked out of one of them. A brief glimmer of hope

arose. Maybe he would smile at her. That was all she wanted, really, something to let her know she was more than a burden. But it didn't really surprise her when he didn't smile, and the hope vanished in the shadows.

"I'm busy, Sally. Whaddya need?"

Her hand went to her hair, and she curled a strand around her finger. She was tempted to flirt with him. Would he open up then, maybe even laugh? Or would he look at her with disgust? Her hand dropped to her side. No, it certainly wasn't worth the risk.

She lifted her chin. "Can I go into town? I wanted to get some more supplies."

He finally stepped out of the stall, and she stopped herself from running over to him and trying to tease a hug out of him. Judging by his lack of closeness ever since they were married, the thought of touching her repelled him. It was too bad she thrived on touch...on feeling the comfort and closeness of another human being. Yes, it was just too bad for sinful little Sally Clay...Clifton.

"What else could you possibly need?" There was a note of exasperation – or perhaps exhaustion – in his voice.

"I... I don't know." She should have thought of that before coming out here. "Umm... Well, I could use some more material for warmer undergarments, what with winter coming on and all..."

"You don't have enough clothes? Use one of yer old dresses."

Her fingers flexed, and she raised her eyebrows at him. "Can't provide for yer family properly?" She hated herself.

Joe's fist clenched around the pitchfork in his hand. "What family?"

"Me! I'm your wife, Joe Clifton."

"And a happy little family we make, huh?"

He shoved the pitchfork against the wall, and it clattered

angrily to the ground. Sally flinched, then turned to leave, rubbing at the burning in her eyes. This was ridiculous. They'd only been married for a little over a month, and they were certainly no more in love than they'd ever been.

A form in the open doorway stopped her from stomping away. Seth looked between the two of them, and to Sally his gaze seemed emotionless – empty of sympathy, just like Joe. But then he said, "I'll take you into town."

She didn't ask Joe's permission. She nodded curtly. "Yes, I'd appreciate that. Thank you."

Joe went back to work without another word.

Seth wasn't the most cordial of company, but Sally understood. She didn't force him to make conversation with her on the long, uphill ride to Virginia City. But when they got close to town, she placed her hand on his arm. "Thank you for bringing me here."

He nodded, his eyes fixed steadily on the road ahead. He looked much darker than his brother, and Sally wondered if it might be the grief. Was grief harder on the countenance than anger and peevishness? Either way, Joe and Seth were not easy to live with.

Neither am I.

Seth pulled up to the general store, now owned by Gray Vercer rather than Jacob Lawson. She shuddered to think of the name of her former boss. Seth remained in the wagon as she jumped down. No need to pretend she was a real lady, not in this town.

"I'll be over at the Delta."

"Suit yourself," she replied, not overly surprised that the man was seeking the "refuge" of a saloon. "I'll meet you there in a few hours."

Again, he nodded, and then he left her there. Instead of stepping into the general store – she'd visit there before she left –

she headed for the Bucket of Blood, another saloon. Scattered whistles and cheers welcomed her, and she was pleased that there were still some regulars who remembered her. To be recognized and appreciated, in whatever way she could get, was a small happiness she couldn't seem to deny herself.

A tall man named Duncan waved her over. "Come sit with me, Sally. I'll buy ya a drink."

"You still dance like an angel, Sally-girl?" another called.

"Things haven't changed that much since I've been gone, have they, boys? Surely you don't doubt my abilities?"

The words flowed too easily from her mouth. She shouldn't be here, and yet she knew she'd never get another dance with Joe. Why not enjoy a couple of turns about the saloon, just to release some of her tension and worries?

"So, who wants to go first?"

"I do."

She spun around, desperate to discover that her ears were lying to her.

They weren't.

Rufus O'Daniel stood in the doorway, his dark brown hair and hazel eyes handsome, but terrifying. There was something about the way his tall form blocked out the light from outside...the way his burning gaze never left her body...the way he managed to stand like the distinguished, stubborn man he was and yet still look slightly bent over, like a mountain lion that had just locked eyes on his prey. She couldn't look away, and she knew there was no way she could outrun his influence. He had been stalking her, hadn't he? And now she didn't have the strength to flee.

None of the other boys protested. If they were in the saloon at this daylight hour, they were in no shape to fight, even if they wanted to, and no one ever wanted to fight with Rufus O'Daniel.

Bert was at his usual spot at the piano, so he started up a

tune. As soon as he started slowly moving his hands across the keys, Sally wished for a faster song, but it was not to be.

Her nightmare pushed her across the room and his grip propelled her toward the dance floor – the space with no tables or chairs – by the piano. His hands locked on her waist, and his glare forced her own hands up to lock behind his neck, which she could just reach without stretching.

Trapped with no key, no escape.

Swaying to the out-of-tune piano music, she longed for Joe. Unfortunately, he was back at the ranch, probably grateful for a day without her.

"I've been waiting for you."

How was it possible that his voice once gave her hope for the future? Such false hope…

She cleared her throat. "Mr. O'Daniel, I…"

"Rufus," he growled.

Licking her lips, she whispered, "Rufus, I think you should know that a lot has changed since I left here several months ago."

With quick movements, he twirled her to his side, her arms tangled in front of her. The side-by-side dance with Rufus had once thrilled her, made her think that maybe she had come to Virginia City for greater things than some poor farm boy with elusive, gold-dust dreams. In the end, the hard, cold realities of Rufus's golden dreams made her long for Jack even more.

"Don't think I'm not aware of what you've been up to." His harsh words pelted her ear as he hovered over her, never missing a step. "You're a foolish girl. Did you really believe that he would want you back? And did you really think that this new marriage scheme of yours would make you happy?"

She winced as he swung her out and pulled her back to him with force, looking down at her with a little grin. "Are you happy, my angel?"

Why was it so difficult to look away, to tell him she was

just fine and he should leave her alone? She was lost, scared of burning the bridge between her and this man who alternately charmed her and haunted her, whose wealth would ensure that she would never be stuck without alternative again. What if things didn't work out with Joe? What if he abandoned her, went east to find Elizabeth or west to find some other decent girl? What if Rufus O'Daniel were her only hope? It was a possibility she couldn't seem to ignore.

She lowered her gaze. "No."

"Speak up, Sally. Are you happy?"

Late nights weeping quietly, wanting Joe to hold her. Days filled with arguments and – even worse – painful silence. Constantly ignored since the moment she said, "I do." And memories of Jack's happiness following her around the ranch like a pitiful stray who just didn't know, or care, that he wasn't welcome.

With a bit more conviction, she told him, "No, I'm not happy, Rufus."

For a moment, as he dipped her to the last strains of the bawdy tune, his eyes were warm with satisfaction. "I'm not surprised," was all he said. But in those words and in his eyes was a suggestion that he held claim to her happiness.

For a moment, she wondered, *Does he?*

And then another shadow appeared in the doorway.

Chapter 15

HE HARDLY LOOKED like an angel, seeing as how he was most likely drunk and certainly shadowed by an earthly grief. But the sudden relief of a familiar face was enough to lift Sally's heart and give her the strength to push away from Rufus.

"Seth! Are you ready to go?"

The darkness of the saloon and his untrimmed beard hid most of his expression from her, but confusion noticeably flickered across his face. His gaze went from her to Rufus to the bar, and Sally realized that he hadn't come here intending to rescue her – he was just hopping from saloon to saloon. He wanted a drink, not trouble.

Rufus stepped around Sally and smiled smugly. "Well, if it isn't Seth Clifton. It looks as if you could use a drink." He stepped toward the bar, apparently confident that Seth would follow. He snagged Sally with an arm around her waist, dragging her along with him and plopping her down on his lap after gracefully taking a seat on a stool.

Sure enough, Seth soon took the stool next to them, his stare vacant as he perused the glass bottles along the wall.

"What will it be, Mr. Clifton?" Rufus gestured toward the shelves. Sally imagined she could fill the one Seth would empty with tears of frustration and fear.

"Seth?" She whispered the name, even though she was sure the handful of people in the building could hear every word.

"Let's go home. I'll fix us supper."

Rufus laughed and tightened his grip. "There's no need to rush off. Plenty of daylight left. We've hardly had a chance to catch up."

Seth traced his finger around a whorl in the wood of the counter. His lowered brows and dark hair in need of a trim hid his expression when he finally looked up and signaled the bartender. "Whiskey."

There'd be no help from Seth. She struggled against Rufus's hold. "Please, Rufus, I need to get home."

He didn't spare her a glance or lessen his hold as he talked with Seth and the bartender. Sally glanced around the room, praying that one of the men would stand up for her. Only Duncan met her gaze, and even he quickly got to his feet, downed the rest of his drink, and left.

Maybe she should just relax. But how could she when it felt like she was being held prisoner? No, if Rufus were the answer to her happiness, he wouldn't make her feel trapped. He would set her free.

Tears filled her eyes, and she suddenly had the urge to knock over every single one of the bottles on the wall and watch them fall to the floor in floods of poison and broken shards. The only glass within easy reach was Rufus's...

Seizing the glass he had just set down, she turned and smashed it against his older, still-handsome face.

The shock sent him backward off the stool, crashing into a nearby table with Sally still in his grip.

Seth jumped off his stool, his mouth agape. The rest of the men in the room stood and stared. But Sally's gaze was fixated on Rufus's face – on the blood dripping from his temple and a cut on his cheek. She couldn't seem to tear her eyes away from the blood. She followed the trek of one little drop that left a trail down to the corner of his mouth, where it became a part of his lips that sneered and demanded, cajoled and seduced. Her vision blurred, and suddenly his lips were bleeding and his face was a pool of blood. She was drowning…

After a quick stop in the general store to pick up some food stuffs and a few other supplies – including a bolt of soft, green cloth he couldn't resist buying for Sally – Myghal had gone to the livery to pay for the use of a horse. He was on his way out of town when the sound of a crash turned his head.

Normally the sounds of a brawl emanating from the Bucket of Blood were nothing to cause someone to stop and ponder. It was the middle of the day, however, and he had been on the alert for any signs of trouble ever since he stepped off the train half an hour ago.

Don't go stickin' yer nose into places it don't belong – there's a lad. Just leave the rascals alone. No sense gettin' involved.

Such thoughts did little good against curiosity. He gave in to the urge to investigate, which was easy enough with his nerves already on edge. As he slid out of the saddle and tied the reins to the hitching rail, he promised himself one peek and then he would be gone.

The promise fled as soon as he glimpsed Sally on the saloon floor in a man's arms, surrounded by splintered pieces of wood. Not just any man's arms – Rufus O'Daniel's. And there was blood.

That blood seemed to fill his entire vision until all he saw was red.

Marching into the saloon, he made a quick scan of the room. Everyone seemed to be in a daze, including a man he was pretty sure he recognized as Joe's brother. He knelt next to the couple on the floor and reached out to pull Sally up. She pushed him away with a cry, scooting back from the unconscious O'Daniel and bursting into sobs.

"Sally, lass, come here. I'll take ye home." It was painfully difficult to keep his voice calm, when all he wanted to do was shout at the men who'd let something like this happen – whatever it was that had happened.

Her crying increased in volume, and he suddenly realized that there was blood on her hands and arms. How bad were her injuries?

Easing closer to her, he laid a gentle hand on her shoulder, swallowing loudly at the brokenness of this lovely young woman. When she didn't lash out again, he pulled her into his arms and cradled her against his chest.

The man whom he thought was Joe's brother stared at them, shaking. Myghal nodded to him. "Seth, right? Were ya the one who brought the lass here?"

Seth didn't respond, looking down on O'Daniel like he expected the man to rise up at any moment and attack him.

"Seth." Myghal bumped the man with his shoulder, careful not to jostle Sally too much. "Go and fetch the wagon, or horses, or whate'er ye came here in."

Another bump with his hip brought the man's tortured gaze to his. Slowly, it dropped down to Sally. Passing a hand over his face, he finally went out to do as Myghal bid.

None of the other men said anything as he followed Seth out the doorway and into the street. When he paused on the wooden sidewalk, Sally shivered in his arms. He bent protectively over her. "'Tis all right, lass."

She didn't meet his gaze or acknowledge his words, and Myghal worried that perhaps she had hit her head in what must have been a rather bad fall.

"Hurry up, Seth," he muttered. Perhaps the man had run off instead of doing what he was asked. Who knew if Seth could even think straight at the moment? He was obviously drunk.

When Myghal shifted Sally's weight to get a better grip, she clutched his shirt in tight fists and pressed her head to his shoulder, as though she feared he would let go.

"Nothin' to fear. I've got ye."

His soothing words made her relax her grip, but she still wouldn't look up.

A wagon rolled in their direction, and Myghal sighed in relief. As soon as Seth brought the wagon close, he lifted Sally toward the seat. She clung to him tighter and whimpered.

He heaved a sigh. "I have to drive the wagon, and I cain't do it while holdin' ye. But I promise yer safe now, and we'll take good care of ya when we get to the ranch."

"I can drive." Seth stayed where he was on the seat, looking straight ahead but giving a slight nod as if to assure Myghal he was sober enough to handle the task.

It was ridiculous to think of letting a drunken man drive the wagon down the steep path into the canyon, but he nodded back, regardless. Prying Sally's hands from his shirt, he placed her on the seat next to Seth, then made quick work of tying his horse's reins to the back of the wagon and joining Sally. With her tucked into his arms once again, they set off for the ranch, Myghal whispering prayers for safety.

Marriage was far from being the safe place for his heart Joe had always hoped for. What had he been thinking, marrying a girl like Sally? He hated himself for wondering how different it would have been if Elizabeth had married him, but every time his mind wandered to the argument he had with Sally this morning, his mind automatically sidetracked to Elizabeth. Her gentle ways, her innocent smile, the way her hair almost shone red in the desert sunlight...

Shaking his head to clear it, he went back to cooking supper. Forget Sally and Seth being home in time for the meal. They were probably having a grand, carefree outing.

The sound of the wagon rumbling toward the house did little to make him feel better. So they were back. He wasn't going to wait for them to care for the horses and wash up before he started eating. Let them take care of themselves. He was through with trying to rescue everyone.

He plunked a plate down on the table and dropped into his seat, his fork poised to take his first bite of beans, when the door burst open. Joe jumped to his feet and dropped his fork with a clatter, startled to see Myghal in the doorway, holding a sleeping Sally in his arms.

She is sleeping, right?

A sudden dread made his stomach clench hard. His hand shook as he reached out to touch her arm – but the glimpse of blood stopped him with a jolt. "What happened? Where's Seth?"

"Takin' care of the horses. Do ya have any bandages?" Myghal appeared to be searching the room, not meeting Joe's fearful gaze.

"Yeah." He rummaged through the shelves, knocking over some cans, which fell to the floor with several loud *clangs*. Curse his wretched hand!

Myghal had settled Sally on the only couch in the main room. After seeing her chest rise, Joe released his own breath and shoved the bandages into Myghal's waiting hands, then set about getting a wet cloth.

"You never answered my first question," Joe growled as he pumped the water harder than he should. He turned his head slightly, wanting to know what Myghal was doing here and why Sally was bleeding and if she was going to be all right.

"I don't really know. I found her in the Bucket of Blood, with Rufus O'Daniel unconscious on the floor and Sally in his arms. You'll have to ask Seth the rest."

"What?" Joe whirled around, the rag dripping all over the wood floor.

No trace of Myghal's usual lightheartedness flickered in his gaze. "There are some things I need to talk to ye about, but first, we should take care of the lass."

That was *his* job. He should have taken care of her, should have taken her into town himself instead of being a stubborn mule of a man. Ignoring Myghal's outstretched hand, he knelt next to Sally and gently washed her right arm, working his way down to her soft palm and her small, delicate fingers that were now cut and scraped.

"It was that O'Daniel fellow."

Joe and Myghal both looked up at the sound of Seth's voice. Seth closed the door but didn't move any closer, looking almost afraid of Sally's pale figure lying on the couch. His hair was all wet and sticking up in places, as if he had dunked his head in the horse trough. Probably had.

"I found her with him in the Bucket of Blood. O'Daniel offered me a drink, so I accepted. Then, for no reason at all, she turned and smashed the man's glass against his head."

Joe looked down, clenching and unclenching his fists, crushing the rag he held in the process. That hardly seemed like the full story, but at least that would explain why Sally's one hand was all cut. His gaze moved up her arm and then back to Seth. "But why are there cuts on her arms?"

"O'Daniel fell off the stool into the table and dragged her with him. I guess the fall must have scraped her up some."

Joe directed his next question to Myghal. "Was she unconscious when ya found her?"

119

"No, but she seemed ta be in shock. She fell asleep on the ride here."

Sally, what were ya doin' in the Bucket of Blood – and with Rufus O'Daniel, of all people? No telling what could have happened to you.

Joe was torn between shaking some sense into his wife and hugging her to his heart and never letting O'Daniel or any man near her again.

Instead, he continued to wash away the blood, relieved to discover that besides some deep cuts on her hand and a few splinters in her arms, she wasn't too seriously hurt. Myghal, silent, handed him a bandage, and he wrapped it gently around her hand. With the last tug of the bandage as he tied it in place, Sally gave a soft moan and slowly opened her eyes.

Pushing aside the urge to berate her, he forced a small smile, which was met with one of her own, until she looked around and seemed to realize where she was.

"Myghal…?"

"Here, lass." He stood, his light eyebrows lowered over his eyes. "Seth and I brought ye back to the ranch."

Joe helped her to sit up and watched as she placed her bandaged hand in her lap, covering it with her other hand. "And Mr. O'Daniel…?"

Joe saw Myghal's jaw work, and he felt his own teeth practically grind in response. What was the story with Rufus O'Daniel?

"He was still lyin' on the floor when we left."

Sally closed her eyes and rubbed her hurt hand. "Is he… Do you think…I killed him?"

A tear slipped down her cheek, followed by several more. Joe joined her on the couch and put his arm around her, urging her to rest her head on his shoulder.

"No, Sally, the man was just unconscious."

"Are you sure?"

"I'm certain."

She buried her face into Joe's shirt before he could tell whether she was relieved or disappointed at Myghal's words.

After a moment of uncertain silence, Myghal declared, "I'll be sleepin' out in the barn, then, if it's not too much trouble. We can talk more tomorrow, I'm thinkin'." He stepped around Seth and walked outside.

The sound of the door closing must have startled Seth, for he jumped a little and shuffled farther into the room. His gaze landed on Sally and Joe, and a shadow as dark as Naomi's grave passed over his face. When his mouth opened slightly, Joe thought for sure he was going to ask something, but no words came out. Instead, he turned and headed to his own room.

Joe glanced down at Sally's tangled golden hair. He longed to ask her about what had happened today, to demand she tell him what was going on with Rufus O'Daniel and why she had gone to the Bucket of Blood. He wanted to punish her for being so foolish, but he held her close and tucked her head under his chin, rubbing his hand slowly up and down her arm until she fell asleep again.

Chapter 16

RUFUS O'DANIEL SAT in his room at the hotel, his old breech-loading rifle lying across his lap. Back during the War Between the States, that gun had made him feel safe – perhaps foolishly so, but at least he was still alive when many of his fellow compatriots were not. At the age of forty-four, he felt less cocky than he used to feel with the rifle in his hands. It was enough to think of all he had survived, all he had achieved…all mocked by Sally's constant rejections. His grip on the barrel tightened. That last humiliation in the Bucket of Blood would not go unpunished.

It was time to eliminate the competition. And if that didn't work, he would eliminate the problem. Love wasn't that different from war. It was time to surprise the enemy, to take the prize and claim the victory.

He'd been on the losing side once before, but not this time. It was all up to him, and he wasn't going to accept anything less than complete and total surrender.

He slammed the door on his way out, the sound echoing like a gunshot in the hallway.

Harsh sunlight slowly flooded the canyon, a hint of promise in the air that had nothing to do with Myghal. This ranch didn't belong to him, nor did any hopeful illusions. He was here to warn Joe so that the man could best know how to protect his wife. Any thoughts of staying nearby as a neighbor and friend to this couple vanished yesterday when he saw how the two of them were struggling. They didn't need the confusion his lingering emotions might bring.

Lost in painful thoughts as he leaned against the corral, he didn't hear Joe until the man appeared next to him, elbows resting on the top of the fence. "I'm sorry we don't have enough room in the house for ya."

Myghal pushed back and ran a hand through his hair, which had started to curl from going too long without a proper trim. "Don't ye worry about it. The barn was jest fine, and besides, I'll not be stayin' long."

Joe turned toward him, brow lowered. "Why did you come?" An uneasy silence followed before he added, "Not that I mind. It's just that Sally and me – we're not gettin' along so well, and I don't know if we're really up for entertaining company."

A sharp tug at his heart pulled Myghal's ready smile down and out of sight. "I understand. I wouldn't 'ave come except that Zachary Taylor told me about Rufus O'Daniel nosin' around, askin' about Sally. I just knew I had to warn ye and to offer help, should ya be wantin' it."

"We already knew he admired Sally." Joe absently rubbed his moustache with finger and thumb as he looked away, toward the horses in the corral. "What makes ya think it's anything more than harmless interest?"

Myghal gripped the top rung of the fence with both hands. "There's nothin' harmless about the man, Joe. Ye know that. Why would he be stalkin' her? Don't ye remember how desperate Sally was to leave Virginia City? And now ye have brought her right back to him."

Joe kicked the fence. "So this is all my fault? You're blaming me for putting Sally at risk? If ya felt this way before, why on earth did ya let me marry her and bring her to my home?" Joe's voice rose with each word, and at the last he pushed away from the fence and leveled a glare at Myghal.

Myghal didn't back down, though a pinch in his chest begged that he face his feelings. "You and Sally need each other, and I'm not questionin' that. I only wanted to be sure ye were aware of the threat." *And I wanted to see the two of ye again.*

But Sally and Joe had started down a different path together, and just like when Elizabeth and David returned to Colorado, Myghal was left to forge ahead, alone. It was as if he had to relearn the lonely art of being an immigrant – of making a new life for himself in a different, initially friendless place – over and over again. Suddenly, he was weary to the very depths of his heart.

"I appreciate that, Myghal." He could hardly tell it from the look on Joe's face. With a shaky sigh, Joe added quietly, "If I can't even protect her from me, how can I deal with Rufus O'Daniel? I think Sally despises me, and I don't blame her."

Myghal had no words of wisdom to share. He had failed at love once, and he doubted he would ever have another chance to claim it. Why did he think he could march right back into Joe and Sally's lives and expect to be of help? A corner of his heart was stuck in a place that understood Sally's desperate cries by the river that horrible day – a place that bled anew every time he thought of his Lydia married to another man.

Myghal gestured to the horses in the corral. "Do ya mind if I take one of yer horses out for a ride?"

The simple question and the suggestion of distance were received like an olive branch, and Joe gave a small smile in response. "Take your pick."

Left unspoken were the words, *And take your time.*

"Is Myghal leaving?"

Sally's expression was anxious as she peered out the window, her face silhouetted in the window's glow and her bright blond hair like flowing sunlight over her shoulders.

"Just takin' a ride. He'll be back in a while." Joe's fingers itched to shut the curtains Naomi had made and force Sally to look at *him*.

"Oh." She turned to him then, her injured hand pressed behind her back, as if she was afraid even the sight of it would upset him.

"Sally." He took a step closer.

"Yes?" She absently rubbed her right arm, and the action brought back thoughts of the previous night. He had sat for a long time with her asleep beside him, until he finally carried her to their room and slept with her curled up against him. It was the best night's sleep he had enjoyed in a long time – when he had simply comforted her and loved her, without excuses or judgment or fears.

"I…" *Love you.* The words died on his tongue before they could be spoken.

He swallowed and tried again. "I don't need to know what happened yesterday."

Her eyebrows lifted in surprise, and her head angled to the side as she stared at him. "But…I thought you would be angry." She brought her injured hand back in front of her, clutching it against her middle, reminding him that he was still rather in the dark regarding yesterday's events.

"I was. I probably still am." He rubbed his sweaty palms against his pants. "I just want to start over. Can we?" For one night, he had caught a glimpse of the sweetness of caring for a wife, of being strong for her, merciful. This one time it wasn't worth rehashing everyone's mistakes.

Her eyes widened, the blue brimming over. Why was she crying?

"Sally? Dear heart…"

The endearment caused several tears to spill onto her soft cheeks. She took one step toward him, hesitant. When he opened his arms to her, she fell into them and sobbed against his chest.

"Oh, Joe..."

No other words came. He smiled into the hair brushing against his chin, reveling in her nearness.

Then a loud *crack* of rifle fire from outside caused both of them to jump.

"Sally, get out here!"

Sally gasped, the noise harsh in the terrible silence that followed the gunshot and the command. "It's Rufus..."

Pushing her away, Joe headed for the door. "*Stay here. You hear me? I don't want you leaving this house.*"

"Don't go out there. He sounds too angry." She threw her hands around his waist, like she was going to use all of her strength to keep him inside. "He's mad that I hit him. It embarrassed him, that's all. There's nothin' for the two of you to talk about. Please don't leave." Her words were warm against his back, almost melting his resolve. "I know him. He isn't reasonable when he's angry."

"Reminds me of someone else I know," he replied, trying to add teasing to his tone in order to calm her. "He has to know that I won't back down." Turning in her arms until she was nestled in front of him, he hugged her close and whispered in her ear. "You're my wife. I will protect you."

"Please don't..."

He kissed the top of her head and then stepped out of her embrace, ignoring her pleas as he grabbed the shotgun by the door and walked out onto the porch, closing the door firmly behind him. O'Daniel was standing several yards away, his rifle aimed at Joe's chest.

"What do ya want, O'Daniel?" The fall wind was cool as it

blew past him, and he blamed his sudden shiver on the crisp air.

O'Daniel nodded toward the house, the gun never wavering. "I want the woman. She was mine for years before you spirited her away, and I want her back."

The man stood as straight and still as a statue of a Civil War soldier. Had O'Daniel fought in the war? Cold sweat slid down Joe's back beneath his shirt, but he wasn't backing down.

He gritted his teeth. "Sally is my wife, not my 'woman.' We are bound together before God and the state, and no one should try to separate us. You may be one of the wealthiest men around, but you can't buy Sally."

"I certainly have more to offer her than you do. Why don't we just ask Sally to come out here and choose the better man?"

The gun was slipping in Joe's sweaty hands, and he wished he could set it down and wipe his palms on his pants again. "So you can threaten her and scare her into going with you? I don't think so. You had your chance to marry her, but that chance is gone. Just leave her alone!"

O'Daniel took a step toward the house without lowering his rifle, and Joe could see his gaze narrow on the window, as if he were trying to see Sally through the glare.

Joe raised his gun, wishing Myghal would come back or Seth would appear. "Don't come any closer."

The bullet slammed into his abdomen and threw him to his back before he heard the report. It came before he could think of a prayer…before Sally's muffled scream reached him through the walls of his childhood home…before he could imagine what his death would mean for the people he loved.

The pain tore at his gut, and a fire seemed to roar to life in every part of his body. He could barely sense Sally hovering over him or hear Seth shouting from somewhere out near the barn.

Oh, God…

Long ago he had prepared for such a moment, but he had never thought it would be so soon, or so violent and unexpected.

Sweat poured from his brow and stung his eyes. *Oh, God, please help! I can't just leave Sally. I love her. Did I ever tell her that? And Seth and Myghal... It hurts so bad, God. Please forgive me. Oh, God...*

When a hand reached out to lead him home, Joe grasped it and breathed his last.

Chapter 17

SETH CLIFTON WAS a peaceful man – or at least he used to be. Anger took a long time to seep into his heart, as did any other deep emotion. His pa had first come to Nevada with his wife and nine-year-old Seth in '60 when news of silver had tempted him to finally strike out on his own, away from the family dairy business. He had been one of the few to build a life for himself instead of following the gold or silver wherever it decided to pop up next, even though it didn't keep him from dying in the desert like everyone else.

So all Seth had known was this ranch, this desert valley with its outcast inhabitants scattered among the sagebrush. He married a local girl – a Jewish woman who wasn't welcome in Virginia City but was as familiar to Seth as the horses and scorpions. He was satisfied with his lot in life. His younger brother and the wind kept him company during the day; stars and his woman kept him company at night.

He never understood why Joe was so restless, why he found a job in town, fell in love with some stranger from Colorado, and then up and left for the forests of the California coast. Not until Ma died, and then Naomi, and now...

Suddenly, the canyon wasn't big enough to contain Seth's rage and grief.

With a yell that would have scared the Rebels in the War Between the States, he stormed up to the porch and grabbed the shotgun his brother had dropped, barely glancing at Sally holding his brother's head in her lap. A lingering look at the scene would kill him, too.

Hefting the gun to his shoulder and pointing the barrel at the demon who had shot his brother, he roared, "Get off my property!"

He fired twice above the snake's head, hating himself for not being brave enough to shoot the man right between the eyes. His arms quivered, and with a choked sob he shouted, "Get. Off!"

The gun barrel shook dangerously as Seth watched Rufus O'Daniel slowly back away. Why couldn't he just shoot him? O'Daniel stared at Sally and Joe with a dazed expression, then turned and started toward the path out of the canyon...away from the evil he had caused.

Seth let the barrel dip before tossing it into the dirt and heading toward the barn, walking away from Sally's weeping and his brother's blood-covered body in her arms.

The tune of the wind whistling through the canyon floated around Myghal, mingling with memories of Lydia's laughing blue eyes and Sally's somber blue gaze...of Lydia's light-hearted grin, and Sally's awed smile at the sight of a hillside full of lupines.

He was happy for both of them. Well, as happy as he could be for Lydia when she promised herself to him and then married another. But at least Sally, who had only ever been his friend, was married to a good man who would give her a good life.

With a glance up to the twilight sky and the specks of silver beginning to appear, he let go of a breath he had been holding in for far too long.

There's a time for everythin', right, God?

He clung to the hope that someday there would be a time

for him to keep instead of always having to learn to let go.

An eerie feeling descended on him the closer he got to the ranch. It was probably due to the tension left over from his talk with Joe earlier in the day. He should have come back from his ride much sooner so that he could leave before nightfall.

A dark shape lay on the porch. Maybe Joe had been waiting for him to return, or...

Finally, Myghal understood. He remembered seeing a mother cradling her grown son's crushed body after he helped bring him up out of the mine. One of the shafts had collapsed. She had crumpled to the ground, too shocked for tears, holding her son in her lap and brushing the hair from his disfigured face. The picture was as cold and unreal as the sight of Sally holding Joe's limp body. He reined in by the barn, then jumped off the horse and ran the last few yards to the house, another deep breath catching in his throat.

"Sally...what...what happened?"

His eyes told him that Joe was dead, but his brain couldn't comprehend it, and his heart wouldn't believe it. He took one step, then two, hesitantly. Sally didn't respond; she just continued to run her small fingers through Joe's hair.

Then Myghal saw it and knew. The blood – it was dried and almost black in the encroaching darkness, but there was no denying what it was. It was all over Joe's shirt and the surrounding floorboards and even on Sally's hands.

Sinking down onto his knees next to the body, he clutched Joe's sleeve, willing him to wake up. This death... It was so sudden and painful and wrong.

"How...?" The word drew tears from his eyes. He lowered his head, unable to even try to meet Sally's gaze.

She was silent so long, he thought she might not ever speak again. Finally, she whispered, "He shot him."

"Who shot him?" As soon as the question left his mouth,

he realized the answer. Rufus O'Daniel. He clenched his hands into fists. "How long ago?"

"I don't know." Her voice was small, fragile, like a child afraid of receiving a scolding. "Hours. Forever."

He finally looked up. She watched him, nothing but misery in her gaze. "It's my fault…"

She began to weep, cradling Joe's head in her lap and clinging to the neckline of his shirt as she bent over him and released heart-wrenching sobs.

Myghal couldn't respond. He stood, his shoulders unbearably tense and his head throbbing with the thoughts he couldn't allow himself to process. He pounded his fists once on the doorframe, his heart shattering into thousands of pieces of broken glass scattered across a sea of darkness that would soon swallow them up.

Chapter 18

SOMETIME DURING THE NIGHT Myghal must have brought Sally into the house and tucked her into bed, because the last thing she remembered of the end of that horrible day was the feel of Joe's blood-soaked shirt in her hands. For a while, she had imagined that he was lying next to her in their bed, his shirt soaked with sweat – not blood – from a hard day's work, and Joe too exhausted and too comforted by her presence to get up and change his clothes.

Sally squeezed her eyes shut tight. He would never lie next to her again. Not even in death.

At some point after…he…left and before Myghal came, she had decided that Joe must be buried in the Virginia City cemetery, among all of the other good Catholics and Christians. Sally would be buried with the outlaws and Jews. A soiled dove could fly about all over the town, but she could never land among the church-goers.

Joe, however, deserved better. He was a respected man with a respectable life, and she would see to it that he got a proper burial.

That goal was the only thing that helped her push aside the blankets and get off of the bed. Padding slowly to the mirror, she brushed and styled her hair, washed her face, and applied some cosmetics. Then she put on her nicest decent dress, which was rather plain but would have to do.

She glanced once more at her reflection in the mirror, and anger filled her at the sight of the calm, silent woman gazing back. Didn't she know that nothing she did would make things right? Didn't that woman know that she would never have a chance to be the wife Joe had deserved? Picking up her hairbrush, Sally aimed at the woman's heartless eyes, her hand drawn back and her thoughts murderous.

The slam of the front door – the sound that proved she wasn't alone – caused her to break her gaze with her reflection. She brought her hand over the dresser and dropped the brush onto it. It clattered in time with the stutter of her heart, and in just the same length of time it took for her white knuckles to return to their normal color.

"Sally? Are ye awake?" Myghal appeared in the doorway, concern quickly flashing to surprise as he took in her appearance. "Sally-girl…"

He didn't finish the thought. He just stared at her with a mix of uncertainty and apprehension that made her long to break something, to do something to release the emotions hidden somewhere beyond her reflection.

"I want Joe to be buried in Virginia City." She pushed past him into the hallway. Finding the front room and kitchen empty, she asked, "Where is the body?"

"I asked a few of the Jewish women if they might help prepare…fer burial."

She felt him come up behind her, and she didn't know whether to turn around and thank him for asking someone else to do the task, or to slap him for not consulting her. Joe was her husband. As a good wife, she should take care of all the details, help him look his best.

Instead, she only nodded. "When will we be going into town?"

He walked around to stand in front of her, his hand reaching out to touch her arm. She pulled back, not wanting any comfort, any contact. Myghal's sigh filled the room like a ghost. She pinched her eyes shut at the thought.

"Don't ye think it best to avoid town?"

His words were gentle, but anger simmered beneath them. For one irrational moment, she wanted to tease the sentiment out of him – to poke and prod at the emotional nest of snakes until he lashed out.

"Joe should be buried up there, not down here."

She opened her eyes in time to catch the curse he mouthed without voice – a sight she never thought she'd see in connection with Myghal.

He swallowed forcibly. "I don't want ye in the same town as that man. As soon as we bury Joe, I think it best if we return to California, at least fer a time."

The front door had opened so silently, and she had been so focused on Myghal, she hadn't heard Seth enter the house, but the force of his glare finally alerted her to his presence.

Seth spoke from the doorway. "And why should we run? If the law won't hang him for murder, then I will."

Myghal crossed his arms. "I'll go into Virginia City to tell the sheriff what happened." He snorted contemptibly. "I don't expect him to be able or willin' ta do much, not when Mr. O'Daniel can pay off anyone he chooses."

At the mention of the murderer's name, Sally gasped and Seth sucked in a heavy breath.

"I don't think it'd be wise fer either of ye to go," Myghal added.

He didn't need to clarify. Everyone knew the danger. And Seth could very well seek to avenge his brother by causing another death. The thought of any more killings terrified her, because if Rufus deserved to die, then so did she.

Sally stomped her foot. "Joe has to be buried there."

The door slammed again, and Myghal was gone.

Her gaze met Seth's, and it was as if she was looking at her reflection again. Why were they burying their emotions? Why didn't Seth yell at her or hit her? Didn't he know that if it weren't for her presence here, his brother would still be alive?

She watched his fists clench and unclench and wished that he would use them, but all he did was walk past her, down the hallway to his bedroom.

For a while, she remained rooted, unsure of what to do. Seth clomped around in his room, his booted steps loud and heavy, but what she most longed to hear was Joe's voice, reprimanding her or laughing or asking her what was wrong. It wouldn't matter what he wanted to tell her or how he wanted to say it. She wished she could remember him saying anything, but the only sounds she could recall were his dying breaths, choked and raspy and filled with pain.

With a cry, she ran to her room and threw her brush as hard as she could into the mirror. Over and over, she repeated the gesture until she drowned out the memories with the sound of breaking glass and the sight of her own cut-up hands. Bleeding, bleeding, bleeding...

The reverberating crash brought Seth's pacing to a standstill. He stared at the door, waiting for Sally or Myghal or anyone else to break it down and shoot him where he stood. For being a coward. For not protecting his home and family. For letting his brother and his wife and everyone he ever loved die.

A moment passed before he realized that no one was coming. He was tempted to stay in his room – any destruction of property was well-deserved, in his mind – but he opened his door and glanced across the hall, to Joe's old room.

Sally sat on her knees, surrounded by pieces of glass, clutching a brush in her hand. She was shaking, but not crying, so far as he could see.

He should leave her alone. What good would his comfort be? Besides, he didn't know how to give it. He had nothing good left to give.

The emptiness of his bedroom pulled him from behind, a force that was powerful, if not welcoming, in its promise of escape. Still, he couldn't look away from the girl and her grief. His mother would have wanted him to do something to help her, quoting some verse from the Bible about mourning with others. His dear wife would have wanted him to be strong, to take charge of the situation and pray to God for all their sakes.

With halting steps he came to her side, the only sounds her heavy breathing and the crunch of glass beneath his boots.

She was Joe's wife. Someone's daughter. My sister-in-law. I have to do something.

He didn't know what he would do with his life in the days ahead, but in this moment, he had a job to do.

As he awkwardly knelt down beside her, the *pop* of his knee startled her and brought her attention to his face. Something familiar in her eyes prompted him to say, "I know."

Together, they cleaned up the room.

The little wooden cross and the solitary location seemed unfitting for a man who had sacrificed so much – a man whose heart, impulsiveness, uncertainties, and hope spoke of so much life to live.

Myghal stood beside Sally, his arms still shaky from the effort of digging the hole in the desert ground for Joe's body. Sally had given up her fight for a Virginia City cemetery plot, which simultaneously relieved him and concerned him. He wished he hadn't had to deny her request, but his trip to Virginia City had only confirmed his fears – Rufus O'Daniel had been a frequent visitor at all the saloons the past few days, and the sheriff refused to investigate any of Myghal's claims about the murder.

Joe couldn't be buried in the small Jewish cemetery in the canyon, either, so Myghal dug a grave a little ways behind the ranch house, close to Joe's mother and father's graves. He wished he could do better for his good friend. He wished so many things could be changed...

The sound of a clump of dirt hitting the wooden casket cut off his ponderings. Sally knelt next to the grave, one of her dirt-dusted hands tracing the words on the cross:

Joe Clifton
1863-1886

"I never thought he would leave me first," she said quietly.

Myghal knelt next to her, and Seth did the same on the other side. The day was still and cold, the heavy clouds threatening rain, or possibly snow. The coming weeks would see the canyon filled with deep and blinding white.

He wanted to say some words about Joe, to help them all somehow, but his memories felt frozen and too far out of reach.

Sally held up a little coin purse, one he had glimpsed her toying with on occasion. "Do ya think Joe would mind...?"

Myghal shook his head. "No, lass." He didn't know what exactly she was asking, but he knew that Joe would've wanted her to embrace healing.

A part of him wanted her to open the tiny bag and show him what she had treasured for so long, but she didn't. She held it tight for a moment, her eyes gazing blankly at the grave as if she were trying to quickly relive all the memories that pouch represented. Then she dropped it onto the casket with the *thump* of a slamming door.

Her lips parted as if she wanted to say something, but she simply stood and walked toward the house, leaving Seth and him to cover the casket with dirt.

As he shoveled, Myghal longed to face the past, to accept the memories and let go of the doubts. Instead, all he could think about was the future – how he could best help Sally and Seth, and how he could keep Sally safe. What would Joe have done if he had realized how serious the danger was?

Seth spoke into the stillness. "I'll help you convince her."

Myghal looked up in surprise. "What do ya mean?"

"I mean that we shouldn't stay here." The admission creased his forehead, a look of painful acceptance and determination. "I know you want us to come with you to California, and I think that would be best. Anywhere away from here."

Myghal nodded, and they shared no more words as they sweated with effort, despite the chill, and finished filling the grave.

Seth wasted no time in heading back to the barn when the deed was done, but Myghal lingered beside the little cross. "I wish I knew what to say, what to do. I wish this hadn't happened, Joe."

He clutched the shovel tight in both hands, the little cross blurring in his vision. Lifting his gaze to the sky, he asked, "Why did it have to happen? Why, God? How could Ye let O'Daniel murder him?"

Throwing the shovel to the ground, he brought his hands to his face, covering his eyes and his tears. "Could I have done anythin' differently?"

He stayed standing beside the cross for a while, until Sally came out and walked with him back to the house.

Part III:

The Causes of My Soul

"O Lord, thou hast pleaded the causes of my soul;
thou hast redeemed my life."

Lamentations 3:58

Chapter 19

SEVERAL MONTHS HAD PASSED since Sally, Myghal, and Seth left Nevada. With the money Seth received from selling the ranch, they bought a small, two-bedroom home and a nearby shop in California, in a little place known as Ferndale, about half a day's journey from Eureka.

The three of them decided on Mended Heart Bakery as the name of their shop. Sally had initially wanted to name it Bleeding Heart, in reference to the little heart-shaped flowers that Myghal had given her on her wedding day. But Myghal suggested a more hopeful name, one that could still allow them to paint flowers on the wooden sign outside of their shop while suggesting that the sweets they offered could ease any heartache.

Myghal had also somehow charmed his way into a deal with Noah Falk. He and Seth would take turns working in Falk's mill, switching every other week, so that one man would always be around to help Sally with the shop while the other man earned additional income as a woodsman. Sally suspected that Zachary Taylor's good word, as a loyal and needed cook at the lumber camp, greatly helped Myghal's cause.

So they all found a routine and started a new life together.

"Did you get more sugar?" Sally didn't look up from where she was making cinnamon rolls. She had forgotten to add sugar to the list, but she assumed that Myghal, with his sharp eye for details in all areas of life, would know they were in need of more.

"Sally?"

Sally's hands froze over the partially rolled dough. His voice rose a bit with uncertainty, but it was still as deep as she remembered.

A sharp feeling in her chest made Sally wonder if her heart was literally cramping with the pain and shock of hearing his voice again. He couldn't possibly be here. He had his own life, and she had hers.

The fluttery feeling that arose within her contradicted the twisting sense of dread wringing her insides. She did her best to keep all of the emotions hidden, but she couldn't look up for fear that one glance would tell him everything.

"Sally, is that you?"

Her resolve to ignore him might have lasted if the door hadn't creaked open once again. He was leaving? She glanced up to find Jack looking at her, his head cocked, while Myghal stood behind him in the doorway, hefting a heavy-looking crate.

"Oh, dear..." The words slipped past her lips because something had to. She worried that the contents of her stomach might soon follow.

"Sally, lass? Are ye all right?" Myghal looked between her and Jack, wariness shadowing his gaze. He shifted his stance, his arms straining as he clutched the crate.

Sally snapped her mouth closed and wiped her hands on her apron. "My goodness! I'm sorry, Myghal. You can set that over here by the cabinets." She gestured to a spot on the floor next to her, behind the counter, frustrated that she couldn't seem to stop her hand from shaking. She went back to rolling the dough, hoping to hide her reaction to Jack's presence.

Myghal slid a glance toward Jack, who remained frozen in the doorway, then did as she asked. When he set down the crate, he stayed next to her, crossing his arms over his thin chest. As much as Sally detested the silence, she couldn't bring herself to say anything to Jack – she had no idea what she could or should say to him.

Finally, Jack asked, "When did you get to California? I thought… I thought you would be back in Missouri with your ma and pa."

Swallowing back the anger she had hoped never to feel again, she squared her shoulders. "I never went back home." She met his gaze then, and found it to be full of confusion.

"It's been over three years. What have you been doing with yourself all this time?"

His tone was cautious, almost hopeful, like he was catching up with an old friend who would give him a brief description of her adventures before they parted ways again. His gaze flicked to Myghal, perhaps expecting a sweet love story. Like the one he had apparently experienced?

No words could sum up what had happened to her since Jack told her to go home and left her to find her own way. Tears filled her eyes, and she started to pound the dough, not caring that it no longer needed the harsh treatment.

"I think ye should leave," Myghal said, his voice tight but sure.

Jack's handsome face scrunched. His brows lowered and his head shook slowly from side to side. "I don't understand. Obviously, something is wrong. Tell me, Sally."

"Tell me your dreams, Sally," he said as he leaned in close, close enough for her to kiss the tip of his straight nose. "Tell me what you want most."

In that moment, the only wish in her head was that he would lean in all the way and press his lips against hers – her first kiss.

Sally shook the memory away as a hot tear spilled down her cheek at her former innocence and her foolish fancies. "Please, just leave," she whispered, brushing away the embarrassing display of emotion as her hand resumed its trembling.

Before Jack could respond, the door opened again, and a young woman entered the bakery.

"Jack? Don't tell me you got sidetracked by all the sweets?" Her voice was laced with teasing and affection. She glanced at Sally. "You'll have to excuse my husband. He can't seem to limit himself when it comes to sugary things." She smiled, bringing a self-conscious hand to her pretty pink hat. When no one responded, she turned to Jack. "Did I interrupt something?"

Sally contemplated escaping through the back door, but Myghal touched his hand to her back, causing her breath to hitch before she took another, deeper one.

Myghal stepped up to the counter. "I'd be happy ta help ye, ma'am," he told Jack's wife.

He packaged up the pastries she wanted, took the payment from Jack, and walked them the short distance to the door, giving Jack no chance to continue their previous conversation. When the door closed behind them, Sally left the battered dough and sank down onto the floor with her back against the counter. All she wanted to do was hide there and cry.

Myghal's steps echoed through the small shop as he came around the counter, sitting down beside her, clasping his hands atop his knees.

"I don't understand," she whispered through tears of shame and hurt. "How can he be here? I thought they lived in Oregon...?"

Myghal didn't say anything. He probably had no answer, just as she had none.

"I'm home," Seth declared as he entered the house, relishing the warmth that filled him at the words. He really did feel at home here. It was good to be in a green place, where the air felt clean and damp, instead of dusty and dry. And it was freeing to discover that he could indeed embrace a life beyond the one he had always known.

"Supper's almost ready," Sally called back from the kitchen.

Seth smiled, surprising himself with his own contentment. There was nothing like coming back to this peaceful place after an exhausting week at the lumber camp. The other woodsmen must hate him and Myghal for their constant reprieves from camp life…but that wouldn't stop Seth from taking them.

He entered the kitchen and sat down at the table, placing his hat on his knee and leaning back with a sigh. "Where's Myghal?"

After placing a bowl of mashed potatoes on the table and rushing back to the stove, Sally hitched her shoulder toward the bedroom he and Myghal used. "In there, getting his stuff together."

Seth nodded and stretched, catching Sally's glance when she came back to the table with a bowl of beans. She gave him a small smile, and Seth found one of his own rising to match hers. He looked forward to a week of working with her at the shop. The smells of cinnamon and baking bread combined with the sweet taste of stolen samples to provide a happy break from the sweat and cursing and trees crashing to the forest floor.

Sally returned with a plate of fried chicken, which she set in front of him with a smirk. "No point in putting this anywhere else. We all know you'd climb over the table to get the first piece."

Seth laughed.

"What did I miss?" Myghal asked as he entered the kitchen.

He looked to Sally with surprise as he voiced the question, his frown incongruous with Sally's cheerfulness. Her overly-bright smile faded at Myghal's expression, and she turned away from the both of them. Had something happened this past week while he was in Falk? Seth wondered.

"Only the usual. I was just making a remark about Seth's hearty appetite." Sally mumbled the words, her voice suddenly tight.

"Ah. Well, while we're makin' remarks about Seth, ye need a shower, man." Myghal sat down across from Seth with a grin.

"As you do every other Saturday, as well."

Sally came and sat at the head of the table, between them, appearing relieved with their banter. Seth resolved to get to the bottom of whatever had happened after supper, before Myghal left. He wanted to be there for Sally. He didn't want to lose the smiles and laughter they had only recently found.

Sally strained to listen to the conversation in the next room, every now and then clattering the dishes loudly enough so that the men would think she was paying them no mind. Myghal was telling Seth about Jack's appearance at the Mended Heart, describing what Jack and his wife looked like and urging him to watch out for her in the following week. Sally would have smiled at their protectiveness if she wasn't so weighed down with heavy thoughts.

Jack. Surprisingly, as much as she detested her reaction to his sudden appearance, she found herself more curious about it than heartbroken, now that the initial rush of emotions had passed. Jack was a ghost from her past – a desire, a dream that had haunted her since his disappearance – but he couldn't hurt her anymore…she hoped.

"Need any help with the dishes?" Seth walked into the room, startling Sally out of her thoughts. His dark eyes held compassion, and it made him look so different from the man she had met when she first came to his ranch. It was as if he was now a warm, fresh loaf of bread, instead of the nebulous, sad mass of dough he had been.

She couldn't help but smile at him, this man who had left everything behind for her and Myghal, for all of them. *Like his brother.* Her smile dipped just a little.

"I'm almost done. You can stack these dry dishes in the cupboard, though, if you'd like."

"Sure," he agreed, reaching close to grab one of the bowls.

"Thanks." She flicked a glance to the other room. "Myghal leave?"

He nodded. For a few moments, they completed the domestic task in silence. Then Seth ventured, "What are you going to do?" He must have seen the denial she was about to voice, because he added, "I know you were listening. The house isn't that big."

She shrugged, placing the last plate in his large hands. "I don't know." Pulling out a chair, she sat at the table, looking down at her lap where she clutched her hands tightly together. "Part of me wants to tell him everything that happened since he left me – about working in Jacob's place. It was what I had been going to do when Myghal and...your brother...and I had gone to Oregon. I wanted him to suffer, and yet a small part of me wanted him to take me back."

A chair scraped the floor and Seth sat nearby, but she didn't look up.

"Everything's changed. I mean, he's married. I got married... And now we're here, and I don't want to think about the past anymore. I wish I never had to think about it again."

Finally, she risked a peek and found herself held by Seth's steady gaze. She licked her dry lips. "Should he know?"

His chair was turned toward her, and his hands were clasped between his knees. She wished he would tell her what he was thinking. Was he remembering his brother? His wife?

Was he contemplating the past, or their future – hers and his and Myghal's?

With a sigh, he leaned back in his chair. "I don't know, either." A shadow crossed over his face before he stood. "I'm going to sit outside for a bit."

She nodded, following him with her eyes until the kitchen door closed behind him. Then she followed his movements with her ears as she heard him enter his bedroom – probably to grab his pipe – and leave the house.

Getting up, she opened the kitchen door, looking between her empty room on the left and the front door ahead of her. Biting her lip, she pondered her choices for only a few seconds before heading outside.

He was sitting on their small porch, smoke drifting around his head and into the evening air. She took the chair on the opposite side of the porch, watching the stars appear in the sky and lamplight appear in their neighbors' windows. The smell of pipe tobacco comforted her, and she breathed a prayer of gratitude for hope, for healing.

If Jack hounded her, she would tell him the truth. She didn't want secrets to shatter what they had worked so hard for. But if Jack let it go, she should, as well. They had both changed. Their journeys these past few years had been so different. Their current destinations, while the same literal place, could not provide a shared lodging for their hearts.

Help me, please, to stop chasing after him, to go back to following Your steps, as my parents once taught me. I don't want to fight anymore for something I shouldn't have. I just want peace.

She begged over and over for God's guidance as she sat before her new home, surrounded by sweet quiet and tangy tobacco smoke.

Chapter 20

WHEN THEY OPENED the bakery on Monday morning, Jack breezed in with confidence and determination.

Seth hadn't seen Sally so fearful since...well, for several months. He clenched his fists, remembering the times that he had done nothing when he should have done something. When he didn't tell Elizabeth her brother's secret. When he didn't try harder to get medical help for Naomi. When he didn't come to Sally's aid at the Bucket of Blood. When he didn't shoot Rufus O'Daniel.

He gritted his teeth and rounded the counter. He was a man well-acquainted with inaction, hiding behind a serious demeanor, acting like the older and wiser big brother he had always hoped himself to be, when he was really afraid of all the terrifying changes his own actions could bring about. Perhaps, all this time, he should have been more afraid of the horrible things his own inaction allowed.

Because change had found him, found them all, no matter how hard he had tried to deny it.

And these recent changes in his life were worth taking action to keep.

Assuming a protective stance in front of the counter, he locked gazes with their customer. "What is it you're needing?"

The man's greenish eyes – like a cat's, or maybe a snake's – darted between him and Sally. "I'd just like to speak with Sally, if she would allow it."

Seth caught Sally's shudder out of the corner of his eye and heard her quietly agree.

"I'll talk with him, Seth."

She sounded resolved, if not happy about the situation. He flexed his fingers in agitation. This man was married, and her relationship with him was long past. He knew enough of her story, and this time he wouldn't sit by and watch a man hurt her.

"Let me talk with him," he said.

He was ready to brush aside her protests, but none came. He looked over to find her close to tears. Her hand shook as she set down the spoon that she had been using to mix cookie dough.

"Are ya sure?" she asked in a murmur.

When he nodded, she gave him one of her sugar-soft smiles, and that was all he needed to steer him toward the door, with Jack in tow.

They walked down the street, passing several shops.

Jack dragged his feet through the dirt. "May I ask who you are to Sally? I saw her with another man last week, and I just assumed he was her husband."

Seth was uncertain how to answer that. He finally decided on a simple response. "I'm her brother-in-law."

"Ah." Jack nodded, as if that cleared up everything.

"That other man – Myghal – he's a close family friend." The words rushed from him before he could think about why it bothered him so much for Jack to assume Myghal was Sally's husband.

"Oh? Then where is her husband?"

They walked past the saloon, and the notes of an out-of-tune piano hit him like the blows Joe should have given him for not whisking Sally away from the Bucket of Blood that day.

Did this man really need to know all of their heartbreak? Unable to stop his voice from deepening with threat and pain, he replied, "Dead."

"Oh. I'm very sorry to hear that."

Silence enveloped them as they left the saloon behind.

When they got to a bench in front of the blacksmith's place, Jack gestured to it, and they sat side by side, watching a wagon rumble past and the sky darken from white-blue to a hazy silver.

Jack's knee bounced up and down, a surprising display of nerves from an otherwise confident, self-assured man. "Look, I know you must be wondering what I want with Sally." He spread his hands, offering a lopsided smile. "I assure you, I'm happily married and I have no desire to bother her. It's just that, well, I got the impression that something was wrong last time I saw her. We were close once, and I wanted to make sure she was all right. Perhaps I was just mistaking her grief for something else." He huffed a humorless laugh. "I don't know what I was expecting to learn."

"When did you and Sally part ways?"

Jack's knee bounced faster. "Well, it was a few years ago. I thought she realized that I wasn't ready to settle down, but unbeknownst to me she followed me from Missouri, all the way to Virginia City. When she caught up to me in Nevada, I told her how it was between us. I told her to go home." His brows rose. "Virginia City was no place for her, you know? I knew she needed to go back to her family and find another man who was willing to make a home for her."

He turned to Seth, and his fidgeting stopped. "Now, will you tell me what happened after that? Because I never thought I would run into her all the way out here."

Seth ran a hand through his hair, grateful he could spare Sally from this recounting, but hating the fact that this man could be so unaware of the tragedy he helped to cause. "She never went home. I'm guessing you already figured that out. I don't know the whole story, but I was told that she didn't have the means to get home. She ended up working on Sporting

Row in order to make enough money to get by."

Jack clenched his hands in front of him, crushing the hat that he had taken from his head moments before. "For...how long?" The question was a whisper, a murmur laced with frustration and fear.

"Almost three years. It's been close to four since you left her, right? It's only in the last year that she got out of that...situation."

Seth rubbed his hand over his knee, wishing he could rub out this conversation. "Last summer my brother and that man you met last week came to California to work in Falk. Sally went with them. It's my understanding that she convinced them to go to Oregon after a while, because she heard..."

"She heard I was there."

"Yes."

"If she came, why did I never see her?"

He sounded wounded, like he needed to know more but was having a hard time bearing up under the pain of the story.

"I don't know."

Jack jumped to his feet, pacing back and forth on the edge of the dirt street. Seth contemplated telling him about Joe and Sally's marriage and their time back in Virginia City, but images of Sally in Rufus O'Daniel's bloody arms...of Joe's lifeless body...of Naomi and Joe's graves...

No, he had told Jack all he needed to, all Seth was able to tell. The memories were still too ragged and raw.

"What can I do?"

Jack's question pulled Seth out of his self-loathing and sorrow for a moment. He shrugged. "Nothing. There's nothing you can do now."

He hadn't meant it to sound so accusing.

Or perhaps he did.

"I don't know how to apologize, how to make this right."

Jack growled in frustration. He must have glimpsed Seth's head shaking slightly back and forth, because he added, "You have to believe that...all this time...I thought she was back home. I knew she had hopes for us, and I did feel bad about hurting her by sending her away, but I knew it was for the best. She shouldn't have been there."

"No," Seth agreed, "she shouldn't have."

Pushing his slightly crumpled hat back firmly on his head, Jack faced him with determination. "My wife Molly and I have done really well in the dairy business – here and back in Oregon. I'll give Sally some money, to help with the bakery."

Seth shook his head again. No amount of money could ever compensate for all Sally had suffered.

Jack's chin lifted defiantly. "That should be Sally's decision, don't you agree?"

It was true. He wasn't the one Jack had wronged. Seth nodded grudgingly. "You're right. I'll tell her about your offer."

"Good. I'll visit the bakery tomorrow." He hesitated for a moment. "Would you...would you tell her that I'm sorry? That I never knew she was still in Virginia City? I know I can't ever make up for leaving her like I did, but I want to do something. I have to do something."

"I understand," Seth agreed.

His words seemed to give Jack some relief, and the man inclined his head to Seth before heading down the street, away from the bakery. Seth dragged the toe of his boot through the dirt, hearing the unspoken words, *It's too late*, echoing around his aching mind.

Rufus O'Daniel tugged his hat down low over his face, simultaneously hating the poor quality of clothes he was forced to wear in order to "blend in" and also feeling like they somehow suited him now. He'd become a common criminal, if murder could ever be "common." Somehow, it all felt so different than the killings he had done in the War Between the States. He shuddered in the chill of the foggy day. He couldn't allow himself to think too long on it.

He only had a few moments to observe Sally through the windows of the bakery, for he doubted those fellows who had just been with her would be gone long. No one left Sally's side for long. Her vulnerability, her sass, her charm – it all kept drawing him back. What was he lacking, that Sally wasn't drawn to him? Well, before murder stood like a barrier between them…

He put a hand to the cold glass. Now she was safe behind the pretty door with "Mended Heart" painted across the sign hanging above it, and he was outside wandering like a brave but stupid fool, where she and her companions could rightly shoot him down.

He almost wished for it. Someone as easily distracted by a skirt as he was, as directionless and pathetic as he was, deserved to be shot down like the lowly volunteer he was in this war he had waged.

And yet an O'Daniel never gave up a fight, no matter how far the war went. Single-minded, dedicated, fearless – that was how he had been known among his fellow Confederates. He couldn't forget that. The memory of his former glory, the reality of the prosperity he had found – that was what defined him. Certainly not gutlessness, nor being bested by a prostitute who didn't realize how much he had to offer.

His head pounded as he continued to watch her work. It was early enough that most of those in town were just now getting up and about, too busy with their own schedules to notice his presence as he stood frozen to the patch of dirt outside her little shop. He didn't have much time to lollygag, and a part of his throbbing mind recognized that he was being ridiculous.

She looked up from where she had finished placing some sort of dough into the oven, and her gaze met his. Even though he couldn't hear it, he could see that she gasped, her startled eyes filling with fear and disbelief.

When had he become the kind of man that women feared, rather than the one they flocked toward?

He didn't shake his head or put a hand to his temple as he wanted to. He simply kept watching her for a moment, taking in her golden hair and the healthy rose-color in her cheeks.

Let her know he was here. Let them all know that Rufus O'Daniel was a man of ambition, of perseverance. If he gave up on this, on what he had wanted so badly for so long, he wouldn't know who he was anymore.

With a nod in Sally's direction, he pushed off the window and ambled away, confidence and determination holding his shoulders back, though his head hung forward.

Chapter 21

WHEN THE BELL above the door to the Mended Heart rang several minutes after Rufus disappeared, Sally whirled toward the sound, dropping the plate she had just finished piling with cookies. The crash reverberated through the small place, bringing her back to the Bucket of Blood and the cut on Rufus's face from where she had hit him with the glass.

"Sally? Are you all right?" Seth looked at her as if she were an abused dog, ready to bite at anyone who came too close.

Shaking her thoughts away, or at least trying her best to do so, she knelt on the floor, gathering the ruined treats and pieces of broken plate into her hands. When she didn't hear anything more from Seth, she glanced up. He stared at the floor, his expression even more serious than usual, as if he were concentrating deeply. Maybe remembering the same scene she had been?

Wanting to spare them both the discomfort, she tried to bring him back to the present. "I'm sorry. You...you just startled me."

It took a few more minutes of downcast eyes and hands carefully piling up the mess before Seth moved into the shop, going to get the broom in their little supply room in the back.

"I'm sorry to have startled you. I hope you don't have this reaction every time someone comes into the shop, or we won't have many customers." His tone was a mixture of humor and wariness, but his gaze was all concern.

She couldn't tell him about Rufus. He would tell Myghal,

and then they might do something drastic. Like sell the shop and their sweet little home. Despite the difficulty of seeing Jack here, she didn't want to leave. She refused to let Rufus O'Daniel keep on taking the things that she loved.

And what about the people I love?

She swallowed, hearing Rufus's voice bellowing at her to come out of the ranch house, seeing Joe crumple to the porch. Dead.

A shiver coursed through her. There was no stopping the tight ball of fear and worry from tumbling out of her. "What do you think of closin' the shop for a few days?" The question slipped out like yolk from a cracked egg.

"What? Why would you want to do that?"

Seth finished sweeping up the mess, while Sally went to the washbasin to clean her hands. How could she convince him to leave? Maybe they could confuse Rufus as to their whereabouts. At the very least, the situation would be easier to face with a plan.

She tucked a strand of hair behind her ear and then rubbed it between her fingers. "It's been a while since I've seen Mr. Taylor. You and Myghal get to see him all the time, but I'd like to visit with him again. And…" She scrambled for another reason. "Well, wouldn't it be nice to have a break? We could go to Eureka, maybe spend an afternoon by the bay or somethin', and then go to Falk. Myghal could bring me back on Sunday." The words were coming fast and desperate. "I could use some time away after seeing… Well…"

She would let Seth come to his own conclusions. Seeing both Jack and Rufus was enough to make her heart quake, her hands tremble, and her eyes fill with tears.

Seth came over to wash his hands, and Sally moved only enough for him to stand in front of the basin. He was so near, and in that moment, so somber. She had seen him change so much for the better in these past few months. What if she became the cause for his smile to disappear forever?

Reaching out a tentative hand, she touched his arm below his rolled-up sleeve, surprised at how cold his skin felt. He turned to her, and she felt a tear slip down her cheek. "Please, Seth…"

He watched the tear's journey as it slowly fell down her face before reaching out to brush it away with his thumb. "All right."

Oh, how she hoped they would be "all right" again…

"How is she doing?"

Myghal pondered Taylor's question as he leaned against the work table in the main cookhouse. What was the true answer? Perhaps only the Good Lord and Sally knew that.

He tossed a potato from hand to hand. "Better, I think. The work at the bakery has been good fer her, an' she seems happier than I've ever seen 'er."

Except for the first time she had seen the ocean, when they had played in the waves like carefree children. Or when they had come across the field of lupines, and her eyes had lit with wonder and pleasure. But those memories were tucked tightly away, to be relived when only he and God could experience and cherish them.

"Good." Taylor nodded. Hefting a knife, he began to peel the bowl of potatoes. "You ought to bring her sometime, maybe to one of the Saturday night dances."

Before Myghal could protest or agree – he wasn't sure which he wanted to do – a voice replied, "No need. Seth brought me."

He quickly pushed off the table and turned to find Sally and Seth standing in the entrance to the kitchen. "What happened?"

Why were they here? Was Sally all right? Who was watching the bakery? The questions swirled through his mind like storm-churned waves of the Pacific.

Sally smiled, although it seemed strained. "Everything's fine. We just decided to close the bakery for a few days and visit you two." She swung her pretty blue gaze to Taylor. "It's been a while since I've been able to annoy Mr. Taylor and mess up his kitchen."

"True," Taylor agreed, never pausing from his task, although he allowed a long-suffering grin to appear on his face.

Sally sidled up next to Taylor, her smile growing as she snatched up a potato and a knife. "I might as well get started causing as much damage as I can."

Myghal looked to Seth, who still stood in front of the door. Seth inclined his head, subtly suggesting they leave – hopefully in order to talk about the reason for this unexpected visit.

Following Seth out the door, he took one last look at Sally, who was laughing at something Taylor had mumbled, appearing more relaxed and happy. He smiled, pleased to see her at home in Taylor's domain. Maybe everything really was fine.

They left the cookhouse, and Seth shot him a glance. "Why aren't you at the mill?"

"It was my turn to give Taylor a hand with the cleanup. I'll be headin' out soon, so be quick about tellin' me why ye and Sally are here."

"It was her idea."

"Does it have anythin' to do with Jack?" It had to be him, since their weeks at the bakery were usually considered a relief from their labor at the lumber camp, and Seth wouldn't be eager to leave.

Seth nodded as he leaned back on the outer wall of the cookhouse. "He came back to the bakery a couple of days ago, wanting to talk to Sally. I talked with him instead. Told him what happened when they parted ways in Virginia City. He wants to give her some money."

"Money? Is the man daft?" Myghal wasn't given to impulsive acts of violence, but he sorely wanted to show Jack what he thought of his offer.

"I know. That's how I felt, too. But it really should be her decision, not ours."

"Is that why she wanted away? Because of what he told ye?"

"No, I haven't even told her yet."

"Then, why?"

Seth shrugged, his eyes shadowed. "Maybe just the shock of seeing him again?"

Myghal looked to the wooded hills behind the cookhouse. Despite the hard work that awaited him in this place, he could understand why Sally wanted to come. The forest felt like a shelter, a pocket of solitude compared to the open spaces of the desert in Nevada – even compared to the open farmland around Ferndale.

"There's something else, though," Seth added quietly.

Myghal brought his gaze down to Seth, raising his eyebrows in surprise.

"When I came back from talking with Jack, she jumped when I came through the door. Dropped the plate she was holding and looked as startled as a wild horse in the sights of a mountain lion."

"Perhaps she was afraid ye were him?"

Seth shook his head. "It was strange. She seemed really scared, more than a ghost from her past should warrant. I don't know – it just didn't seem to fit. She wasn't sad or upset. She was *afraid*, although she tried to hide it, and that was when she suggested coming to Falk for a few days."

"Maybe all o' the work, and seein' Jack again…maybe she

jest needed a break."

"Maybe," Seth agreed.

But the look they shared suggested that both of them were going to keep a watchful eye on Sally.

Sally shone when she danced. She spun around with a glowing smile, laughing at her missteps and at the words the woodsmen spoke to her. Seeing her open up made Seth want to laugh, too.

He wondered if his brother had seen her dance in this very same place. Was that when Joe had fallen in love with her? When he had decided that he would marry her?

Woodsmen crowded the dance hall. Scattered among them were a few wives and the other workers who made the lumber camp into its own little town. The atmosphere was freeing, thrilling. Myghal was playing a boot-stomping tune on his fiddle, a permanent grin on his face. His red hair whipped about in his skilled frenzy, and some pieces stuck to his sweat-soaked forehead. Seth smiled at the man's obvious joy.

As the song came to an end, Seth suddenly wanted to be a part of it all. It was entertaining to watch everyone else having fun, but how would it feel to actually be involved in the movement and excitement?

Pushing his way through the milling dancers who were waiting for the next song to begin, he found Sally thanking her previous dance partner. She scanned the room, probably looking for the next in line from her admirers. For a moment, he hesitated, wondering how horrible it would feel if she declined his offer to dance.

Before he could weigh the risk, Sally's gaze alighted on him, and she whisked across the floor toward him. Her smile was so bright, he couldn't help but laugh.

"What? Do you find me amusing?" Her tone was accusing, but she didn't stop smiling as she pulled him to the area where two lines were forming. "It's the Virginia Reel – you'll love this!" She practically pushed him into the men's line as she took her own place across from him.

The women's line consisted of several men, as there weren't enough women to go around. Seth considered himself lucky to have Sally as his partner, especially as he watched her clap her hands and bounce on her feet in enthusiasm. She was a different person on the dance floor. But then, she was a different person anywhere now than she had been in Virginia City, despite the encounters with Jack.

Seth followed the men's line and Sally's instructions, content to let her correct him with her cheerful laugh when he tried to pass her by the left shoulder instead of the right. As the dance progressed, he felt warmth spread through his limbs – not just from the exercise, but from the embrace of joy. Naomi would have wanted him to trust in God, to be grateful for the place and the life that he had found.

Seth had only seen Naomi dance once. He had come across her in the barn when no one else was around. When he saw what she was doing, he hid in the shadows by the entrance before she could spot him, enchanted by his wife's movements and the carefree happiness on her face. She sang a song in Hebrew, swaying and spinning from stall to stall as she fed the horses and swept up the loose hay. Her long, dark braid had started to come undone, and she looked more alive and beautiful than anything he could remember seeing.

Now he wished he could relive that moment. He would step out of the shadows and dance with her, instead of heading back to the house to fix whatever it was he'd been working on. Nothing could have needed more attention in that time than his precious wife.

"It's our turn, Seth."

Sally's exuberant voice brought him out of his meandering thoughts. Unsure what she meant, he startled when she grabbed both of his hands and started sashaying with him down the space between the men's line and the women's. When he looked up into her eyes and saw her brilliant smile, he smiled right back and took charge, skipping sideways in time to the stomping of the men's boots. He even twirled her around when they got to the end of the lines, before they had to sashay back up.

He might have missed his chance once before, but he wouldn't make that mistake now. The door to his heart stood wide open, and Sally was dancing him out of the shadows.

Chapter 22

SUNDAY EVENING CAME too soon. Sally and Myghal were almost to Ferndale, and she still hadn't told him about seeing Rufus O'Daniel. Should she? Shouldn't she? She kept swinging back and forth between the two options, just as she kept shifting in the rocking wagon, wondering whether silence or words would be best for them all.

"Somethin' bothering ya, lass?" Myghal glanced at her out of the corner of his eye.

Before she could blurt out the worry weighing on her heart, he added, "Is it Jack? I know this must be hard for ye, seein' him this way."

Yes, she supposed it was, but not as hard as it had been that first time, in Oregon.

She picked at several loose threads in her dress, not sure how to respond. Would her silence or her words unravel all that they had established here? What if Rufus attacked Myghal or Seth? If they had to move again, it would be nothing compared to losing another person she loved to Rufus's obsession.

"Myghal, there's something I have to tell you." She noticed his fingers curl a little tighter around the reins, but she pushed on. "I saw Rufus – Mr. O'Daniel – last week. A couple of days before Seth and I arrived at Falk."

"What?" He looked at her then, his brown eyes fastened on her face. "Are ye sure it was him?"

She wished she wasn't, but there was no mistaking Rufus O'Daniel, even if he had traded his fancy clothes for some common ones. His possessive gaze followed her even into her dreams. She lowered her gaze. "Yes, I'm sure."

"Why didn't ye tell me sooner? Seth and I could've discussed our choices, how best to defend one another. I'm sure Taylor would've helped us."

Tears stung her eyes. She fumbled with her sleeve, attempting to pull out her handkerchief.

"Sally, lass, don't cry." He brushed a gloved hand gently across her cheek, then reached around to rub her shoulder.

"I-I know I should have…told you sooner. I just don't want everything…to change."

He was facing forward again, but Sally could see a wry grin lift the side of his mouth. "It would've changed sometime anyway, ya know, but it won't go back to how it was for ye in Virginia City. Ye don't have to fear that."

She did fear it, though. She didn't want to be that person again – the one who destroyed her own life by making foolish decisions and wallowing in self-loathing and pity. That girl chased after a boy who didn't want her and frustrated the husband who had ultimately been willing to sacrifice everything.

"What if these changes don't last?" She started to sob, unable to hold back the revulsion she felt deep in her spirit at her own weakness, her own shame. Its power surprised her. Hadn't she buried it with Joe's body?

Myghal directed the horse off of the main road, onto a field outside of town. Jumping out of the wagon, he came around to her side, lifting his arms up to her. Through her blurred vision she looked down on his compassionate, freckled face – so innocent and good. How was it that he had ever chosen to be her friend?

She shook her head and lifted a hand to her mouth, shoulders shaking and cries escaping. Myghal lightly touched her arm before he started to pull her toward him, finally urging her to let him lift her out of the wagon.

"Come with me," he said, grabbing her hand and leading her across the field, down toward the Eel River, which they had recently crossed. His grip was strong and comforting.

When they reached the river's edge, he let go. Rubbing furiously at her weak tears, she looked down at the rocky shore and the water moving steadily along. The dairy farmers had all left the fields for the day, and other locals were probably eating supper by this time. It was quiet, peaceful. Just her and Myghal. *And God?*

"I'm so sorry I didn't tell you sooner, Myghal. I'm just so scared…"

How could she explain all of her fears – the jumble of worry for her friends' lives; of losing the Mended Heart and their sweet little home with the white trim and the pretty curtains and the porch from which she could watch the stars; of this affection developing between her and her deceased husband's brother?

Glancing over at Myghal, she saw the pain etched on his generally happy and always accepting face. He must have felt her watching him, for he looked up after a moment and held her gaze. His features relaxed a bit, and she heard him let out a deep breath. Bending down, he picked up a stone and then stretched his arm back before sending it sailing into the river.

"Livin' in fear ain't truly livin'," he finally said. "How can ye find any joy or purpose in the moment if yer always afraid ye'll be losin' it?"

She pondered that for a moment before reaching down to pick up her own stone. "But how can I truly enjoy anything if I know it won't last?" The pebble felt cold in her fingers as she rubbed it back and forth, causing grit to fall into her palm.

"'For here we have no continuing city, but we seek one to come,' so said the author of Hebrews."

"You're speakin' of the Scriptures?"

"Aye. Ya won't find the stability yer seeking here."

She clutched the pebble tightly in her fist, imagining the dirt staining her hand. Part of her wanted Myghal to say more, to tell her that none of this was her fault, that she wouldn't be to blame if everything fell apart again. The other part of her heart cried out to the silence. *I'm so stained.*

Dusk settled around her shoulders as she lifted her gaze to the hills beyond the river. She craved a lasting quiet. She wanted a place to call home where her shame wouldn't haunt her, a place that no one could destroy.

Don't you remember?

The words whispered to her heart, the comforting sounds of a fire crackling and Myghal's fiddle-playing and the ocean murmuring. She breathed in and imagined that she could smell the smoke from Seth's pipe.

Forgive me, Jesus. She mouthed the words, even as she remembered praying them with her daddy years and years ago. She had known the hope of home then, of love and safety...of knowing deep within that nothing, no matter how dark, could take away that love that filled her heart.

I do remember.

Thoughts of Joe's murder crept into the moment, making her cringe with the contrast. But Joe had known God, hadn't he? Not even Rufus's bullet could have taken that away.

Sally opened her hand to look at the hard little rock she had been clutching. A second later, she threw it as hard as she could, watching with satisfaction as it arced through the air and sank into the clean water.

Myghal came to her side, his presence steady and calming. "It's gettin' late. Shall we head home then, lass?"

"Yes." She brushed away the last traces of her tears and gave him a small smile. *It's not too late, after all.*

Chapter 23

SALLY WAS ALONE in the Mended Heart when Jack returned. Myghal was out getting supplies and gathering orders from local restaurants, but he had asked Grant, the blacksmith, if he would look in on Sally when he could throughout the day.

She had trained herself to stop jumping every time the bell rang, but her traitorous heart still raced a little when she saw Jack standing in the doorway, looking more unsure of himself than she had ever seen him. His beard was trimmed, and his face had filled out in a handsome, mature way since their parting. *Yes*, she realized, *we've both changed, and I don't really know him anymore.*

Straightening her shoulders and praying for strength, she got up from where she had been crouching to refill the shelves on the customer's side of the counter. "Hello, Jack."

He dipped his head in greeting, but he didn't raise his eyes. "I've been tryin' to find you."

Her heart seemed to stop before it sped up again in recognition. She had closed the shop the day after Seth talked with Jack, leaving for several days without notice. He must have wanted to speak with her since. "I'm sorry. I...something came up, and I had to leave for a few days."

He nodded again but didn't reply. She considered seeking refuge behind the counter and waiting until he got up the courage to speak, making it as hard as she could for him, but the whole situation between them had been such a horrible mess for too long. It was time to let it go.

She stepped toward him. "I can close the shop for a few minutes, if you'd like. Our house is just down the road a ways. We could sit on the porch."

Was it an inappropriate suggestion? Would he think she was trying to win him back, seduce him? She cringed at the thought.

Forcing her hands to stay clasped in front of her, instead of reaching up to play with her hair to get rid of some of her nervous energy, she waited.

"Yes. That would be fine. If you're sure you can step away for a bit."

She surprised herself with a smile, and gestured around the empty room. "I think all of these customers can wait."

He smiled then, too, and reached out to hold the door open. Before she slipped out she put the "Closed" sign on the inside of the window, then walked with him down the street.

They remained quiet as they traversed the short distance to her house. Despite the familiarity that lingered between them like a low fog, it started to dissipate in the afternoon sun. It didn't hurt to walk beside him, to know that he belonged to another. They didn't really know each other anymore, not as they were now – just the memories of who they once were a long time ago.

When they reached the house, she left Jack to get settled on the porch while she went to make some coffee. It was never warm enough here to offer something cool to drink, and she remembered his fondness for the stuff. Hopefully he still liked his coffee strong.

Finally, she went outside and offered him the mug, then sat in the chair a few feet away from his. She looked beyond the houses across the street, finding a sense of calm in the view of low green hills and cows dotting the fields.

"Your brother-in-law, he told me about what happened after…while you were in Virginia City."

Her hands clenched in her lap, and she tried to relax, letting the rare blue of the coastal sky distract her from unwanted memories. "You don't have to say anything. I know it wasn't your fault, not really. I was foolish."

"I should have made sure you were taken care of, that you made it home safely," he said, leaning forward but still not looking at her. He appeared to be studying the porch planks.

"Maybe," she agreed. But if he had, where would she be now? To never have known Joe…or his brother…or Myghal…or Zachary Taylor…

"I made my choice, Jack, without asking you what you wanted. You weren't responsible for me. We weren't even promised to each other."

"Not in so many words, but I gave you hope."

He had given her that, for a while. "I did blame you for a long time." He was silent, waiting. Did she really want to let him know how deeply foolish she had been? "I… I wanted to find you. I wanted to make you pay. Or make you take me back."

"I heard that you came to Oregon."

"Yes." She would never be able to tell him the depth of sorrow, shame, and hurt she felt when she had seen that he was married. Only God and Joe and Myghal would ever know it.

Jack's knee bounced. "I want to do something, to help you out now."

Myghal and Seth had prepared her for this. "It wasn't your fault." She was surprised to realize that she meant it.

"I didn't handle things right." He ran a hand through his dark hair and stood. "I know I can't make it up to you, but let me give you some money. For your future."

Since I didn't help you back then, was left unsaid but understood between them.

He finally met her gaze, and his was pleading. She had never seen him look at her in that way. In their brief relationship before that wretched trip to Virginia City, he had always looked at her like he knew how desperate she was for his affections. She had been the one pleading – he had been the one obliging, even though he had still been tender to her, at times.

"I don't know what to say. It won't change the past, you know." As he frowned, she hastened to add, "I'm all right. God has been merciful to me." Somehow, she knew those words were true.

"Please, Sally." He sat back down again, facing her this time. "If not for your sake, then for mine. My wife and I have been blessed with plenty. Let me share some with you – for you and your family."

My family. Did he mean Seth and Myghal?

"I…"

"Please."

It felt wrong to accept payment for something that could never be made right. Well, maybe something right could come of it, but that was God's doing, not Jack's.

And yet, she could do this. For Jack. For Seth and Myghal. For her future. A gift to help her in the days ahead, whatever they might bring.

"That is very generous of you. I accept your gift, but I do have one condition."

She had to smile at his hesitant expression. Jack never did like for someone else to have the upper hand. "I'd like for you and your wife to come have dinner with us sometime."

It was her turn to hesitate, unsure if she was expecting too much. Surely, Jack's wife would know what Sally had once been, what she'd done…

Biting her lip, she added, "If your wife wouldn't be offended, that is."

His smile reappeared, and he had never looked so charming. To her heart's relief, though, she found that such charm didn't hold her captive anymore. It only made her happy for their peace, and for his marriage.

"We would be honored to be your guests. Thank you for the invitation."

He extended his hand, and she shook it with a sense of hope and finality.

It had been a month since Sally had talked Seth into that trip to Falk. He cherished the memories of their day on the shore, just talking and watching the boats come in and out of the bay. Their dinner together at a hotel in Eureka, sleeping in separate rooms that night before heading to Falk the next day. Watching Sally dance and eventually joining in her laughter and cheer. Those memories comforted him when it was his turn to endure a week as a lumberman at the Elk River Mill, and they deepened his joy when he returned to her in Ferndale.

Now it was Wednesday, and the thought of leaving on Friday for another week at the mill without her made him start planning. Could he talk her into another short trip to Falk, for the Saturday night dance?

He glanced over his shoulder at her, where she was mixing batter for a cake. She was humming a tune, gazing at the wall like she was lost in a memory. Maybe she was remembering the dance, too? Or was he being ridiculous for thinking he could be on her mind? They were both only recently widowed. It hadn't even been a year since Naomi died. Were his thoughts dishonorable?

Sally glanced over at him then, and he quickly looked down at the loaf he was supposed to be kneading, embarrassed to be caught staring.

"Something on your mind?"

He could hear the teasing in her voice. Was she flirting with him?

When he looked at her again, she blushed. "I'm sorry. I... I didn't mean..."

"It's fine." He knew how difficult some habits were to lose. He couldn't hold it against her because he couldn't help but feel a slight warmth in his chest at her attention.

He saw her nod, appearing contrite and perhaps grateful, before she resumed humming and stirring.

It only took another moment of building anxiety before he felt he had to say something. "There was...is...something on my mind, actually." He folded the dough one last time before he turned, his back against the counter. "Would you like to go to Falk again?"

She held the bowl in front of her and continued mixing the contents, which were probably over-blended at this point. He smiled, feeling his own strange mix of nervousness and anticipation and shame.

"This weekend?" She seemed surprised, but hopefully not dismayed.

"Yeah. We could leave tomorrow, if you wanted to go. But you don't have to – it was just an idea. I thought perhaps we could go to the Saturday night dance..."

He crossed his arms. His words were pouring out like he was an awkward boy, not a widower who was thirty-six years old. Better if he kept the rest of his blabbing and blundering inside.

She laughed, and the sound made his insecurities evaporate. He chuckled, too, and that only made her chortle louder and harder. She set the bowl aside and put her elbows on the counter, her head bent over in her uncontrollable mirth.

"Are you crying?" he asked between chuckles, amused to see her wiping the corners of her eyes with the back of her hand.

"I…can't…help it!" Her laughter had turned to a strange mix of halting giggles and happy sobs.

"I think I should be offended that you found my suggestion that hilarious."

She took a towel from near the sink and fanned her face with it.

Shaking his head, a smile still tugging at his lips, he went back to the dough, shaping it and getting it ready to put in the oven. Just as he slid it on the rack and closed the door, he heard her say, "I think it's a great idea."

His heart stopped, then pumped warmth through his whole body. He straightened and met her sweet blue gaze. "If you're sure."

"Yes. We'll have to work extra hard today, but I don't mind. I love dancing." Her hands waved as she talked, showing her excitement.

"Me, too."

She smiled brightly before spinning around, back to her baking. His throat tightened, and his eyes burned with unexpected tears – perhaps not of laughter, as Sally's had been, but far from tears of sadness.

At the Saturday night dance, Myghal shook his head, partly to move his unruly hair out of his eyes, and partly in amusement at Sally and Seth's antics. It was obvious the man was smitten – and when it came to dancing, he made up in enthusiasm what he lacked in skill. The wild-hearted Sally and he made quite an intriguing couple on the dance floor. They were a lot easier on the eyes than the woodsmen forced to dance with one another for lack of women.

He directed his concentration back to the song he was playing, trying to match tempo with the other musicians. He could get carried away with the fiddle – swept away in a fast-paced song about a man who had made fast-paced, rash decisions and thereby lost the woman he truly loved.

For a moment, he wanted to throw down the fiddle, take his turn with Sally, lead her around the room and spin her into his embrace. He would show the world that he was a man with dreams of his own, with a heart that could win another's. He could.

Couldn't he?

There is a time for everythin'. I jest wish I knew when the time for keepin', and lovin', and embracin' will be fer me.

Was it now? He had wondered briefly if now was that time for speaking up and making a claim. The only answer he really felt to the prayers he had uttered while loading logs for the Gypsy locomotive to transport or while assisting Sally in the kitchen was a nagging restlessness. Much as he wanted to be angry with Seth for stealing Sally's affections away, he knew she had never really belonged to him. His heart had confused a true friendship with other sorts of longings. It just wasn't time yet.

For him.

He couldn't deny that Sally and Seth were doing nicely together. As he drew out a high note, he thought of how they both were healing, blossoming like two stems of a lupine plant reaching their petals out to each other and up to the sunny sky.

He grinned. That was the trouble with a lonely man – he ended up filling his head full of poetry and other impractical thoughts.

Reining in his mental wanderings, he brought his fiddle to his side as the song came to an end. Zachary Taylor approached the small, roughly built stage, while the rest of the room hummed with conversation and raucous laughter.

"Is it time again fer another of yer sad songs?" Myghal asked in mock distress. Taylor gave him a pointed look, and Myghal laughed.

"Some of us need a break from your loud and wild tunes."

"Not likely. A dance such as this one is no time fer melancholy, man. Surely the boys will start another civil war if ye insist on bringing down their good mood."

Taylor shook his head, but Myghal could see he was struggling to conceal his grin. "Move out of my way and I'll pretend you didn't just suggest skipping your break."

Affecting a frustrated sigh, Myghal stepped to the side and swept his hand in a welcoming gesture. "Put it that way an' I find I could use a sad song or two. Feel free to entertain those restless boys the rest o' the night."

Smiling brightly, Myghal stepped from the stage and went in search of water. His throat always burned after the Saturday night dances. He did tend to get carried away with the music.

Sidling to the table set with refreshments, he picked up a cup and gulped down the liquid. Lemonade. He grimaced at the sourness. Ah, well. It would only take a few sips to bring him some relief.

Taylor had started singing another war ballad or some such song, by the sounds of it. Scouting the room and not finding anyone he really wished to talk to, he settled against a wall.

After a couple of minutes, he realized that he couldn't see Sally anywhere in the dance hall. Or Seth, for that matter. Had the man taken Sally outside? Clutching the tin cup tight, he formed a few choice words for Seth if he was disrespecting Sally in any way.

As if his uncharitable thoughts had thumped Seth on the head, Myghal saw the man enter the room, scanning the dancers with eyes wide with consternation. Alarm pumped through Myghal's blood. When he pushed away from the wall, Seth seemed to catch the movement and forged a path toward him.

"What is it?" Myghal asked as soon as Seth was close enough to hear him, through a throat now tight with worry. "Where's Sally?"

"I don't know. We finished the last dance, and Sam came over to talk. We were discussing our schedules and the bakery, and… I don't know… Nothing important. It was only a few minutes, but I never noticed that Sally had left. I was just outside checking to see if she was getting some fresh air, but I can't find her." His voice was edging toward panic. "I don't know where she is, Myghal."

O'Daniel. Neither of them needed to say the name aloud. It had been over a month since Sally said she saw him…but what if the man really was here, and he had been watching them, following them, biding his time?

Thrusting his cup onto the table with a clatter, he turned to the doors. Before he and Seth could make it outside, though, Taylor was beside them. "What's happened?"

"Sally's missin'."

Taylor's face tightened. He was aware of Sally spotting O'Daniel weeks ago, and he most likely knew better than either of them the kind of damage the man could do.

"I'll gather some men."

"Good."

With that, Seth and Myghal raced outside. Sally was alone somewhere out there – possibly with the man who had killed her husband to try to get to her.

Chapter 24

"As I see it, Sally, you have two choices. You can either live with me as my wife or go back to D Street and your life as a whore."

Sally struggled against Rufus's hold, twisting violently and trying to bite the hand covering her mouth. She had only wanted to step outside to breathe the cool air and let it refresh her overly warm face. But Rufus had come upon her so unexpectedly that he had already dragged her several feet away from the dance hall before fear sank in and snapped her into action.

Despite the gray that peppered Rufus's dark hair, he was still as strong as she remembered. The muscles he had built up during his years in the Confederate Army must have never been allowed to diminish with disuse. He dragged her to a horse he had tethered a little ways into the forest. With vivid clarity she recalled Rufus's possessive manner toward her when he came to visit her at Jacob's place. He'd always been rougher than many of the other clientele, pinning her down so she couldn't fight back at his harsh treatment. She shut her eyes tightly, terror choking her as, in her mind, she once again saw the tender brown and blue bruises and the rips in her flashy dresses.

What would she do if he dragged her right back to that desperate place, where she traded her body for the provisions needed to stay alive?

When he removed the hand from around her waist, she shoved him as hard as she could and took off running. Before she could scream for help, he pushed her from behind, sending her into the dirt and moss. With his knee in her back, he pressed a cloth into her mouth and tied it tight behind her head.

She rolled over, and he allowed it, adjusting to straddle her. Something sparked in his eyes then, a moment of hesitation. A battle between desire and uncertainty warred in his copper gaze, and she used the moment to try and buck him off. She swung her arms, hoping to connect a punch or a slap.

Anger swiftly edged out whatever else she had seen, and he grabbed her wrists hard. Scowling, he removed a rope that hung from his belt and tied her hands together. No amount of thrashing seemed to distract him from his purpose.

He abruptly stood and yanked her up with him, pulling on the rope so that she was on her tiptoes as he brought her face close.

"I've fought too long and hard to have you, and I will not let you best me."

He spun and headed back to his horse, tugging her along after him. She dug her feet into the ground and finally fell to her knees, hoping to delay him. When they reached his horse, he calmly told her, "You can either ride with me or be dragged along behind the horse. It matters little to me."

He bent down to lift her up. She shook her head and refused to let him. His slap shouldn't have surprised her, but the unanticipated sting still caused her eyes to water. In a matter of moments he had her rope tied to the saddle and was mounted on the horse's back. He took off at a brisk pace, but the gag smothered her cry as her knees skidded along the ground. Finally, she found her feet.

She had to run to keep up, and it wasn't long before her legs felt like they would buckle beneath her.

Maybe he won't be able to get me to Virginia City. Surely no one would let him force me to go with him. No one could make me marry him, and I would only have to tell one person the truth in order to be rescued. I have money now. I have friends who will help me.

The thoughts beat around in her head as she stumbled along behind the horse. It was a drop of sweet hope in a night full of horror. This wouldn't be like it had been before, with Jack. Seth and Myghal would find her. Wouldn't they?

Oh, God. I couldn't bear being abandoned again. I can't go back. Please! I can't go back.

She couldn't remember when she started crying, but the effort hurt her throat and made it harder for her to breathe around the cloth in her mouth. A blackness deeper than the night edged into her vision, but as it brought her once again to her knees she thought she heard the burbling of a river and a whisper.

Don't you remember?

Rufus O'Daniel reined in his horse when he saw Sally fall to her knees. Jumping down from the saddle, he muttered a curse and untied the rope from the saddle horn. He strode over to where she had collapsed onto the ground – unconscious – then eased her onto her back.

Her moonlit hair had come free and now fell across her face in tangles. He fingered a strand, wishing he had the time to show her tenderness, to comfort her, to woo her in a place where he was the only man around.

Something inside him clawed desperately, trying to get him to think through what he was doing. He felt his heart shredding, bleeding, despite the barricade he had fortified it with when making these plans.

But if a man thought too long and hard about the personal

cost of war, he would most likely lose the guts to keep fighting. He had witnessed men desert the Army because they had seen too much blood, too much suffering. He had seen what unpreparedness and fear had done to the Union Army at First Manassas – had watched them flee like cowards. And he had watched the reactions of his fellow soldiers when they came across the devastation of their land, their pride and hope, caused by Sherman's abominable "March to the Sea." They had wept like babes. It should have made them fight harder, but instead many of them crumpled in despair.

Not him. Rufus O'Daniel had channeled his rage into destroying the Union Army. If enough men had been at his back, the war might have gone another way.

This might not be about land anymore, but it was still about pride and hope. He would not be swayed by ugly sights and damaged hearts.

Sally was far from ugly, though, despite the streaks left on her face from tears and the red around her eyes and mouth. When she was his, then he would have the rest of their lives to rebuild and heal. But healing couldn't happen until the war was over.

He brushed her hair from her face and then lifted her into his arms. He brought her to his horse, settled her into the saddle, and kept her there with one arm while he swung up behind her. This was how it ought to have been – Sally welcoming his attention, willingly going into his arms as they rode off together to begin the life he had dreamed for them ever since he had first been with her. She was an intoxicating mix of stubbornness and vulnerability, sweetness and fire, shame and flirt, desire and innocence. Her desperate position made her easy to sway. Some buried hope she clung to made the chase challenging. It stood to reason that the victory would be that much more thrilling. And he was almost there.

As he navigated through the forest, her head listed against his chest. He relished the warm feel of her. He would protect her: keep her from falling, from ever going hungry again, from ever having to share of herself with anyone other than him.

It would be a long ride tonight, but tomorrow they would be married and sailing away from all the troubles she had known here.

Somehow this little sprite had brought him to his knees, but soon he would be the one standing, and then he'd finally have the triumph he had been fighting to claim since the defeat at Appomattox.

Sally struggled, something in her fighting for awareness, and something else wanting to accept whatever darkness surrounded her. The thought of opening her eyes scared her, but she couldn't remember why. She pried one eye open to a slit. She was in a room she didn't recognize, but the vague similarities to Jacob's place made her shudder. She wanted to scream, but the cloth was still in her mouth, and the end of the rope that had made her wrists raw was now tied to a bedpost.

She tried to stand, but the rope was tied to the bottom of the post, and it wouldn't go beyond the frame supporting the filthy, tobacco-juice-spattered mattress. She could only make it to a semi-standing, hunched-over position. The rope must have been shortened since…

Thoughts of Rufus stopped her mind in its tracks. What had happened? The last thing she could remember was following after his horse, growing weaker from panic and fatigue until she slipped into blackness. How had Rufus brought her here? And where was "here"?

Terror rose up in her throat. She fought to stifle it before the gag forced her to choke on it. There was no way he could have brought her all the way back to Virginia City. This had to be some other saloon or brothel. In Eureka? Where would he take her next?

She wasn't going to wait around to find out. Staring at the bed, she tried to figure out how she could escape. Maybe if she could wedge herself beneath the frame...

Scrambling beneath the closest edge of the bed, she tried to get her knees under her so she could lift the frame. If she could raise the post a couple of inches, perhaps she could slide the rope off.

She pushed up with as much effort as she could muster, moaning at the stiffness of her muscles and the pain it generated in her lower back. It wasn't working. Still, she kept trying, only taking a break to try to maneuver the rope farther down the post.

Suddenly, the door creaked open like the lid of a coffin. She whipped around. Rufus looked surprised, probably to see her awake and moved from where she had been slumped against the far wall next to the headboard. Her heart pounded, and she tried to scoot farther under the bed, for what little good it would do. She tugged on the rope, wishing she could find the strength to break it...wishing someone would come and cut it and release her from this nightmare.

He crossed his arms. "What do you think you're doing? You're acting like a foolish child."

And what about you? The words couldn't be released, but she found her fear momentarily replaced by anger. Why did he keep coming after her? Why couldn't they both move past that horrible moment in time when they had both been part of something so wrong, so tragic?

"Get out from under there. We need to leave."

I'm not leaving with you! Oh, how she wished she could tell him. Instead, she moved as far back beneath the bed as she could, until the rope tightened around her tender wrists.

Rufus slammed the door, and a tremor coursed through her. She closed her eyes, wishing she could shut out this room, this man. At a tug on her rope, her eyes flew open. He was cutting the rope from the post. When he had sawed through, he took the end and gave it a jerk, trying to drag her out. She crawled back as far as she could and curled her left foot around the back post, anchoring herself under the bed.

He swore and yanked harder, causing her to wrench her foot. Her cry came out as a whimper. When she saw him let go of the rope, relief coursed through her – until she felt a tug on her throbbing foot. He was pulling her from behind, and her surprise and the pain in her foot gave him the advantage he needed to drag her free.

Panic heated her face. She scrambled to push her dress down from where it had bunched up around her thighs. Before she could think of a new plan, Rufus hauled her to her feet and shoved her into the wall. Her head hit hard, and it took a moment for her to focus on the wavering image of his frustrated face. There seemed to be a hint of weariness in his stance, though, and she thought if she could only find the right moment, maybe she could make a run for it…

His hands bit into her arms. "Enough games. You will do as I say." He didn't include a consequence, but he didn't need to. She could well imagine the things he would do if he let his rage consume him.

She started to shake, and she watched his expression change in response. The few wrinkles on his face became more pronounced, and his eyes softened slightly. "Sally, surely you must realize the kind of life that I can give you. Let me show you what I can offer. When you're mine, these drastic measures won't be necessary."

Unless I tried to escape again. Or if I did anything to displease you. She resented the cloth cutting into the edges of her mouth and keeping her from attempting to reason with him, to share her piece even if he didn't accept it. Not being able to speak made her feel sick, and she tried to swallow, disheartened at the dryness of her mouth and the rapid pulse she could feel due to the tightness of Rufus's grip.

The sound, or maybe the refusal in her eyes, brought hardness back to his hazel gaze. "You'll see."

He let go with one hand and reached for something in his pocket...another cloth. She glanced from his face to the cloth in confusion. But when she felt his other hand relax a bit, she lurched forward. Whatever he had planned was not something she wanted to wait around for.

She felt his arm come around her head as soon as she gripped the door handle in her still-tied hands. The cloth he stuffed over her face was damp, and she struggled in panic, afraid at the weakness seeping into her head and limbs. She pulled on the door with her last bit of energy, and it opened. Shoving her elbow into Rufus's stomach, she stumbled out of his grasp, tripping through the doorway and landing on her knees in the hallway.

Cotton floated through her head, stuffing her ears and her mouth and muddling her thoughts. But she recognized Seth's deep voice, coming to her as if she were underwater. Her heart sped as she tried to lift her head.

I have another choice. Please, God, let there be another choice. No matter what, I'm changed. I can't go back. I won't go back...

Chapter 25

SETH STARED IN SHOCK, his heart pounding furiously. Myghal and a group of the woodsmen had been left behind to continue searching the forest around Falk, in case Rufus had decided to hide out there for a time. Seth and Taylor had gone ahead to search the saloons and check with the men who ran the stage in Eureka, hoping to catch Rufus O'Daniel before he could leave the area with Sally.

Despite his hopes, Seth hadn't been prepared for the reality he now faced. Seeing Sally stumble into the hallway, a cloth stuffed in her mouth and her hands tied tightly together, made him feel sick. What had O'Daniel done?

"Sally!" He lifted the rifle Taylor had thrust into his hands last night. Something seemed to flicker in her expression, but as she started to turn her head in his direction, O'Daniel dragged her in front of him, holding her like a shield. He aimed a pistol at Seth's heart.

"Sally is coming with me. I suggest you don't interfere, Mr. Clifton, unless you want to join your brother."

The words were cold. O'Daniel's mouth twisted in a grimace, as if he found them distasteful.

Seth winced at the reference to his brother's violent death, and he imagined that the blood pumping hard through his veins was also pumping into his vision. The hallway narrowed, a red, angry haze shrouding the terrible scene.

Sally whimpered, her eyes widening as she met Seth's gaze. She was trying to tell him something by her intent stare, but he looked away. He couldn't be distracted. He wouldn't let her pleading sway him.

His hands shook, but he aimed the rifle at O'Daniel's head. Could he shoot O'Daniel before O'Daniel shot him? No one should have to suffer at the man's hands again...

Unwillingly, his eyes found Sally's. She looked terrified, and tears were coursing down her pale cheeks. She was twisting in O'Daniel's arms, shaking her head, trying to reach her hands up. To remove the rag in her mouth?

There was no way he could aim straight – he was trembling too hard, and Sally was making it impossible for him to make sure he wouldn't hit her if he tried to shoot O'Daniel. He lowered the weapon, his pulse slowing to a hesitant thud.

Oh, God. I'm not this man. I don't want to be this man. Please...what would You have me do?

Sally...

His head jerked when he realized what she was trying to do. O'Daniel had her in a one-armed grip – and she was attempting to knock the weapon from his hand.

"Sally, stop!"

He pictured Joe's body in her arms, lifeless and blood-spattered, as he charged across the short distance between them.

God, please protect Sally!

His heart shouted the prayer as he rammed into the two, causing O'Daniel to stumble before falling onto his back.

Seth struggled to pin the man's arm, which was waving wildly. Images of his own body in place of Joe's flitted in and out of his mind as he tried to control the pistol. If he was going to die today, it would be as his brother had – protecting Sally.

Throwing his full weight on O'Daniel's arm, he gripped the pistol in both hands. O'Daniel wouldn't let go, but his hold seemed to be getting weaker...

Suddenly, another pair of hands reached down and yanked the pistol away from both of them. Seth scrambled to his feet, his gaze jumping from Sally, who was squirming in O'Daniel's arms, to the man who had interfered. The proprietor he had questioned just minutes before now held the pistol aimed at him.

"This man paid good money to be left alone." He gestured to O'Daniel, who had somehow found his feet while keeping an arm around Sally's waist.

Seth lifted his hands, his mind filling with a cold fog. He had to do something, but he couldn't think of any solution through the thick cloud of memories and fears. "I…"

He glanced over at Sally, remembering the day he had let her fend for herself in the Bucket of Blood, when the glass had shattered and she had fallen to the floor in O'Daniel's embrace.

He nodded toward O'Daniel. "This woman doesn't belong to him. Look at her. He's forcing her to go somewhere she doesn't want to go. Can't you see…?"

The proprietor shook his head stubbornly. "I see plenty of things in this place. The men pay me to mind my own business. What they do with their whores is none of my concern."

"She's not a whore! She's my brother's widow."

The proprietor shrugged his shoulders, but the gun never wavered. "It's yer word against his."

This can't be happening.

Seth watched helplessly as O'Daniel dragged Sally down the hallway, coming up beside the proprietor. He wouldn't get far, not when it was obvious Sally was being abducted, but the thought brought no comfort.

Please, God. Please. Please. Please.

The silent prayer stuttered in time to the beat of his heart.

Sally's heart was shattering like glass. Seth had tried to rescue her, but he was outnumbered, outgunned. If Rufus succeeded in getting her out of Eureka, what would happen to her? Would Seth blame himself? And what about Myghal and Mr. Taylor?

Seth stared after her, his gaze fiercely intense and his jaw locked. She pictured his appearance when she had first come to the ranch after marrying Joe – his eyes red from tears and lack of sleep, his clothes and hair rumpled. She could still remember the smell of alcohol on his breath, more sour than the soothing scent of his pipe tobacco. Would he return to that state when she was gone?

Rufus pushed her through a door, into a storage room stacked with clutter.

"Why do you have to cause so much trouble?" he growled, taking out that wet cloth again. She guessed it was doused with chloroform – and she wasn't about to let him render her defenseless, incapable of protesting or fighting back.

Grabbing the neck of a bottle between her tied hands, she stood on shaky legs.

Rufus looked shaken himself. "Come on, Sally. It won't be long before we can put all of this behind us."

Stepping back along the wall, she swung the bottle against a crate. It broke with a crash, the contents spilling out like a flood of tears upon the floor. She held up what was left – the neck and part of the top of the bottle, now with jagged edges.

"Sally, do not defy me. We need each other – do you hear me?"

His control seemed to be dripping away like the rest of the wine from the bottle. The hint of pleading underlying his demands reminded her of the desperation, the longing, the false hope that had brought her west in the first place. What would have happened if Jack had never married – if she'd found him single but still determined to push her out of his life? How far would she have gone to get her revenge, or to get him to take her back?

She felt tears dripping off her chin. *I'm so sorry. For how far we've all gone. For how desperately we've wanted our own ways.*

Suddenly, she realized that Rufus was standing before her. The bottle slipped from her hands, her mind registering the loss of it too late. He towered over her, but he didn't take advantage of the moment like she thought he would. Instead of grabbing her, he slowly reached out with his free hand and stroked the hair hanging over her shoulder. She saw him swallow with effort, his eyes still blazing but his hand trembling with some held-back emotion.

"We'd be a perfect fit. You need me." But when his gaze met hers, she saw the words his pride wouldn't let him say aloud. *I need you.*

The door burst open without any warning, and Mr. Taylor stood in the entrance with another man, both pointing guns at Rufus.

The second man declared with authority, "You're under arrest, Mr. O'Daniel, for kidnapping…"

She didn't hear anything else. She collapsed to the floor among the shards of glass and the sad remains of broken hearts.

Chapter 26

SUNLIGHT FLOODED THE FLOOR of the marshal's office. Seth traced his boot through it, then slouched further in his chair as his mind wandered.

He had told the marshal all he knew about the crimes O'Daniel had committed. At times, it had seemed impossible to try to describe what he had seen. How could he convey the shock of seeing the life violently slammed out of his younger brother? How could he express the agony of seeing Sally suffering? And then there were things the marshal didn't need to be told, but they were still a part of the horror – like the blood stains on the ranch-house porch and Sally's bleeding hands. The three of them kneeling beside Joe's grave in the late-autumn cold. Sally's nightmares – and his own.

"Mr. O'Daniel will stay in jail tonight, and I'll wire the sheriff in Virginia City tomorrow regarding the murder of Joe Clifton," the marshal said, glancing between Seth and Taylor. "I'll talk to Mrs. Clifton and that Cornish man you mentioned tomorrow, as well. From what I've seen and what you both have testified to, I think it's safe to say that there'll be a hangin' soon."

Seth felt sick. All he wanted to do was go back to the hotel and see Sally, make sure that she was still sleeping soundly and that the owner's wife was checking in on her as she'd promised.

The marshal stood, fingering the brim of his hat. "I'm sorry for what you've all gone through. It's a real shame."

Yes. So much shame. O'Daniel had done terrible things,

but the shame didn't entirely belong to him, did it?

Seth and Taylor stepped out of the building that housed the marshal's office.

"I'll be heading back to Falk, then," Taylor said. "If I see Myghal, I'll send him along. And I'll tell the boys that the search is over." He sighed deeply and gazed across the street, his eyes filled with some indescribable emotion despite the familiar confident stance he maintained.

Seth nodded absently, held back from rushing to the hotel by something he didn't understand.

Finally, Taylor spoke again. "It's not right, what's he's done to Sally and your brother. He of all people should know that there are consequences for every decision a man makes."

Seth glanced at him sidelong and saw that Taylor had closed his eyes.

"We all had a difficult time accepting defeat, but Rufus never seemed to be able to get his mind and heart out of the Confederate Army. First, it was the silver. Then Sally. They became his new battles to win."

Taylor opened his eyes and turned to meet Seth's gaze. "He lost. Again." His fingers flexed, and his throat convulsed. "It's just a sorry mess. I wish it could have been different."

Clenching his fist, Seth bit back the words that rose as a reflex. After a moment of silence, he said, "I think we all wish many things to be different than how they are."

"Yes, well, I suppose wishing doesn't change another man's choices."

Taylor stepped off the wooden sidewalk and into the street. Turning back, he added with a slight tremor in his voice, "Make good choices, Seth. And take care of her."

Seth glanced into the afternoon sun, letting it mask the reason for his watering eyes. He gave a sharp nod. By the time he looked back to where Taylor had been, the man was walking down the street and out of town.

Seth made his way to the hotel, pondering the tragic friendship of two men who had once fought for the same cause. He had some choices of his own to make, but who was to say he wouldn't succumb to the same selfishness that had engulfed O'Daniel? Who was to say he hadn't already done so too many times to count?

God, I'm so weak. I want to be strong – for Sally, for my friends. Show me the way?

Weeks had passed since Sally's abduction. Myghal's heart had raced when he came across Zachary Taylor on his way out of Eureka. The cook had told him the grand news of Sally's rescue – and the bittersweet news that O'Daniel was in jail, awaiting his sentence. His heart had pounded with worry when he'd first knocked on Sally's door at the hotel, then sped with relief when she opened it with a small smile. His heart had throbbed while he held her hand as she sobbed on the day of O'Daniel's hanging. Now, finally, it seemed things would at last settle back to their old routine.

But while his heart's beating had settled, his heart's restlessness had not.

It was Friday night, and Sally was bringing plates of some sort of cake with strawberries on it to the table, where Myghal and Seth were still digesting the delicious supper she had made.

"This looks great, Sally," Seth said, not waiting until she sat down before forking a bite into his mouth.

Myghal and Sally shared a smile. She was a great cook – and she would make Seth a great wife. It wouldn't be long now before Seth proposed, he guessed.

Myghal took his own bite, swallowing down the sweetness

before saying, "I won't be goin' to Falk tonight, or tomorrow."

Sally glanced up, surprise sparkling in her blue eyes. Her head tilted a little, asking a silent question.

"Taking Saturday off?" Seth voiced his question between forkfuls of cake.

"Yeah."

What he didn't tell them yet was that he would be taking every other day off, as well – at least from that job. He rubbed his hand across the rough wood of their kitchen table, knowing he would miss this companionship, this feeling of belonging. And yet this wasn't his home.

Sally and Seth would urge him to stay, even after their marriage. They were a family of sorts, and that truth made him smile. He wouldn't hesitate to accept their offer, except that he felt a longing in his gut to go somewhere. Thoughts of Cornwall, of the voyage across the Atlantic, of the westward trek with some Cornish friends, of the dangers and excitement of mining in Virginia City – they filled his mind and made him want more.

Not that what Seth and Sally and even Taylor had to offer was not enough. He simply realized that he wasn't ready to settle. When he did, he wanted it to be with a wife and children of his own.

After they polished off dessert, while Sally was cleaning up the kitchen, Myghal gestured to Seth to follow him out onto the porch.

Myghal closed the door and leaned his shoulder against it. "I'll be headin' out tomorrow."

Seth squinted in confusion. "I thought you said you weren't going to work."

"I'm not. I'm leavin', Seth."

Seth sat down on a chair, crossing his arms. After a moment of contemplation, he finally asked, "Where will you go?"

"I don't know. Maybe I'll go to Eureka, see if I can join a crew goin' out to sea. Or maybe I'll head up the coast a ways."

"If you don't know, why don't you stay for a while?"

Myghal turned to look out at the darkening sky, imagining all the places he had seen, and all the places he had yet to see. "It's time. I'm ready ta go somewhere new."

"Is it because of me?"

Glancing back, Myghal could see the shame on Seth's shadowed face. "What do ya mean?"

"My feelings for Sally."

Myghal grinned. "Naw, I know ye two will be good fer each other."

A smile of relief crossed Seth's face. "I want to ask her to marry me."

"I know."

"Won't you stay for the wedding, if she'll have me?"

A wedding could happen within a few weeks, or it might be months. Myghal shook his head regretfully. "Ye know I would love to be there, but I'm eager to be on my way."

Seth stood and joined Myghal on the edge of the porch. "I understand. You know we'll both miss you."

"And I'll miss ye."

Seth offered his hand, his dark eyes lightened with a mixture of kinship and wistfulness.

Myghal took the offered hand in his own and shook it firmly.

"If you ever come through this way again, we'd be happy to have you visit."

Myghal smiled again. "I'll remember that." Then, turning to the door, he asked, "Do ye mind if I speak to Sally fer a moment?"

Seth nodded in agreement, then sat and tilted the chair back.

Myghal entered the house. He found Sally still in the kitchen, wiping the table with a wet rag. "Sally? May I speak with ye?"

She looked up and gave him a wide smile. "Of course." When he didn't sit down, her smile faded a little. "Does this have anything to do with your not going to Falk this weekend?"

Myghal watched her as he gave a slight nod. Her blue eyes looked darker than normal in the dull lamplight, filled with a sad knowing.

She let the rag slip from her limp fingers. "You're leaving, aren't you?"

He wasn't entirely surprised that she had guessed. They had shared a long journey this past year, from Virginia City to Oregon and back, finally settling on the California coast. But it was more than the miles – it was the shared memories and the longings for past love, for future hope. It stood to reason that they had come to understand each other, to anticipate each other's emotions.

"I'll miss you, Myghal. You've been a better friend than anyone could deserve." She sank down into a chair, her eyes brightening with unshed tears. "How can I ever thank you for all that you've done for me?"

He cut her off with an uplifted hand. "I've been blessed by our friendship, too. Yer strength inspires me. Yer healing gives me hope."

"But I've been such a burden."

"Never say so, lass. I don't regret any of it."

A tear fell down her cheek, and she swallowed with difficulty. He reached out his hand, his palm facing up as he rested it on the table. She placed her hand in his, giving him a small smile.

She had touched his heart with her beauty and long-buried innocence. As he stood, bringing Sally up with him, he clung to the peace they had both embraced by the Eel River mere weeks ago. The words he had shared with her, the look of release on her face, had given him the perspective he needed to move forward.

"Let's go join Seth. I bought me own fiddle last time I was in Eureka. We'll sing our cares away."

"I'd like that," she said as she left the kitchen. When he walked out onto the porch a few minutes later, he noticed that Sally had brought Seth his pipe. He smiled at the homey smell of tobacco smoke. It reminded him of his father, of his home in Cornwall.

He began to play a generally fast tune, one that was interlaced with longer, melancholy notes. It was a song about traveling, about crossing the ocean to find a new life in America. It was a song about bittersweet farewells and an insatiable desire for adventure, for freedom.

He grinned as he looked up to the stars, ready to go wandering once more.

Chapter 27

"SETH CLIFTON, are you trying to ask me to marry you?"

Sally relished the baffled look on Seth's face – the way his head tilted as he looked up at her, and the way his lips parted slightly, as if she had caught the words right before he had been ready to speak them.

She wanted to tease him, but it was only a matter of seconds before a smile bloomed on her face. It reflected on Seth's handsome face, bringing his lips together and lightening his redwood-brown eyes.

He looked so good, so different from that day Joe had first brought her to their ranch. His eyes looked clear. His cheeks and chin were clean-shaven, and his dark hair was neatly trimmed. Even as he knelt before her, he looked more confident, and certainly more at peace.

She held her hand out to him, and he took it.

"Since you already know the question," he said with a deeper-than-normal voice, "what's your answer, Sally Clifton?"

She laughed. "Don't call me that! It sounds like we're brother and sister. That would never do."

"No, you're right. What was your last name before...?"

"Clay. Sally Clay."

It couldn't be very comfortable there on the hard wooden floor of the bakery. She decided to take pity on him. "And yes, Sally Clay Clifton accepts the proposal of marriage from Seth Clifton, former rancher and now business partner," she said in as serious and stately a voice as she could manage through her mirth.

Seth got to his feet, still holding onto her hand. She looked up at him, her breath sticking in her throat at the sight of him standing over her. He still had his vulnerabilities. The wounds to his pride and his heart were still healing. But the light of hope in his eyes gave him a look of strength that made her want to fall into his embrace.

So she did.

"I love you, Seth."

His arms came around her, holding her close as she rested her cheek against the rough fabric of his shirt. "I love you, too," he whispered into her hair.

She grinned as she pulled back a bit, but faltered when she saw that Seth wasn't smiling anymore. "What is it?"

"It's just... Do you think it's too soon?"

She cleared a spot on the counter. When Seth saw her struggling in her attempts to get up on it, he lifted her. Sitting on the edge, she stopped his hands from completely pulling away, holding them in hers. She met his gaze.

"I know it hasn't yet been a year since Naomi and Joe died. If you're unsure, I'll understand if you want to wait."

He squeezed her hand. "I'm not worried about me so much as I am about you. I want to do this right." He paused, then added, "I still love her. I cherish my memories of our marriage, and I'm looking forward to seeing her again, in heaven."

"Oh, Seth. I wouldn't ask you to forget her."

It took him a moment to voice his next question. "Would it be hard for you to marry me, knowing I'm his brother?"

She glanced out the window at the bustling people on the street. A sense of purpose filled her. "No. It's hard knowin' that he died trying to save me. I didn't deserve his love. But we were both hard-headed, weren't we?" She glanced back at Seth. "I wasn't the wife I should have been to him. Everything was still so raw."

At the look of confusion on Seth's face, she went on. "I'm rambling, aren't I? I guess what I'm tryin' to say is that it wasn't perfect between Joe and I, and I don't expect it to be perfect between us. Joe was a good man, and I will always be grateful for what he gave me, for all that he did for me, starting with the day he let me come to California with him and Myghal."

She let go of one of Seth's hands so she could touch his cheek. "I miss him. It will be beyond joyous for all of us to be together again."

"So are you saying you don't resent me for missing Naomi?"

"I could never resent you for that. But I'm also saying that there's room in our hearts for each other, right? For all of us?"

Her hand still rested on his cheek, and he reached up to cover it with his own. "Yeah. Through God's grace, there will always be enough love."

She couldn't wait any longer. She reached out her other hand to frame his face, then leaned forward to kiss him. His fingers encircled her waist as he kissed her back. After a moment she pulled away slightly, enough to see his closed eyes and the smile only a breath away from her own.

The sky outside the window was a familiar gray, but the atmosphere in the bakery was pure sunshine as Seth lifted her off the counter and spun her around before setting her on her feet. Held in his arms, Sally was surrounded by love.

Epilogue

SETH AND SALLY sat on the edge of the river, warmed by the rays of the midday sun. Sally dangled her bare feet in the water, her hands behind her as she smiled up at the bright, late-summer sky. Seth glanced at his wife, happy that they had decided to take this walk and enjoy their lunch out-of-doors.

Eel River was a nice place to relax. Perhaps next time he'd bring his fishing pole. Perhaps someday they'd bring their children here to play.

Sally glanced over at him, her hair shimmering like the rays of sunlight on the water. The happiness of his thoughts must have shown on his face, because she responded with a smile that made her eyes squint and her cheeks seem even rosier. He smiled back, reaching out to brush some loose hair behind her ear, then sliding his hand down to hold hers.

They sat that way for a long time – neither one saying a word, neither one needing to.

Thank you, God.

As long as he lived here on earth, Seth knew his fragile heart would probably break many times over. But he was reminded that the journey and the destination were worth it with each new healing and each tender moment, like this one.

Discussion Questions

1. What are some of the different definitions of love presented through the various characters' actions and attitudes? Which character resonated with you the most?

2. Were you surprised when Joe and Sally got married? What did you expect their marriage to be like? How could Joe or Sally have acted differently in order to make their life together more peaceful?

3. When you finally "met" Jack, was he different than you thought he might be? What did you ultimately think of him?

4. Which setting was your favorite—Nevada or Northern California? What did you like about it, and how do you think it challenged or brought out the best in the characters?

5. Were you happy/satisfied with the outcome of the book? Would you have chosen differently if you were Sally?

Author's Note

I believe that love is a journey – as is the experience of reading a book. Thank you from the bottom of my heart for joining me on this particular journey! It is my sincere desire that it blessed you in some way.

The characters of BLEEDING HEART go through quite the journey of their own, traveling from Nevada to California to Oregon – all places that have stolen my heart and my imagination.

My interest in Virginia City, Nevada began sometime in high school. It was that place that really kick-started my novel-writing dreams. Despite the fact that the town is now a tourist trap more than anything else, its history is still preserved in a way that has utterly captivated me. I ended up writing an extended essay on the town while I was in high school. It seemed smart to get a big assignment done *and* to do research for my first (and, eventually, my second) novel at the same time.

Over the course of several summers, my family and I paid short visits to Seven Mile Canyon Ranch (the area where I set the fictional Clifton ranch) and Edith Palmer's Country Inn, doing all of the touristy things like taking a stagecoach ride (via TNT Stagelines), visiting the museums, going on a tour of a mine, walking through the Silver Terrace Cemetery, etc. All of those things served to inspire me…but it wasn't just the usual activities that made me fall in love with the place. It was the out-of-the-way sites, like the Hebrew cemetery in the canyon. It was the atmosphere, some sort of secret thrill charging the air. And it was the people, who make Virginia City an exciting and interesting place to visit even today. If you love all things that have to do with the Wild West, you might want to stop at this little town spilling down the hillside above Reno. I'll always be glad we did!

I should also note that some of the Virginia City establishments mentioned in this book were (and are) real businesses. The Bucket of Blood, the Delta Saloon, and the Washoe Club all existed in some form or fashion in the late 1800s and all remain to this day. I confess to letting my imagination have free reign when it came to describing the Bucket of Blood as I wanted it to be in 1886, though. And whether or not it was actually called by that name back then is possibly debatable (although not necessarily improbable). In any event, the name fit and I'm sticking with it!

As for Falk, I'm afraid you can't visit that town anymore – it no longer exists. There's nothing quite as haunting as walking along a trail where a town used to be and seeing hardly any evidence that it was ever real. The signs along the trail at Headwaters Forest Reserve (not far from Eureka, California) sparked a curiosity within me, and I knew I wanted to write about the logging town that once was. If this book has made you curious, too, I highly recommend FALK'S CLAIM: THE LIFE AND DEATH OF A RED-WOOD LUMBER TOWN by Jon Humboldt Gates. I found a copy at the visitor center at Prairie Creek Redwoods State Park, and I'm so grateful I bought it. It proved to be a helpful tool as I edited this story, and it served to stir the fascination I already had with the town's history.

Finally, my family and I have gone on many a summer trip to Sunriver, Oregon. I couldn't help but include a brief scene there, and it's quite possible the area will serve as a setting for a future book. A family vacation doesn't get much better than rides along their many bike trails, dinner on Mt. Bachelor, canoeing under the stars, and visiting the High Desert Museum (another place that helped me with my research).

The various settings of BLEEDING HEART were like characters—they had personalities and moods all their own. But the actual characters stole my heart, as well. Several of them have been "alive" for me for years. They all have touched me deeply and, through their stories, allowed me to explore my own questions about heartbreak, grief, hope, and love. I hope they came alive for you, as well, and somehow challenged or encouraged you.

If you'd like to learn more about BLEEDING HEART – view some book extras, discuss the story, ask me questions, and more – please visit *www.bleedingheartnovel.blogspot.com*.

Acknowledgements

When you write a story and your heart bleeds all over the pages, it can be a messy and vulnerable thing. You wonder if you ought to let others see. You wonder if others will understand the heartbreak, if they will love the characters the way you do, if they will still support your passion even when they don't understand.

BLEEDING HEART is my second manuscript, and some of its characters are familiar faces from that first story I wrote. To those who read FORGET ME NOT and offered their thoughts on it – thank you. There's nothing quite like that first time you finish a manuscript, and I'm grateful for those who shared the journey, celebrated with me, and nurtured my love for writing. And to those who have shared the journey to publishing BLEEDING HEART...

MY FAMILY. My grandparents, my parents, my uncle, and my sister – thank you for supporting me. I love you all so much! Thank you, Mom and Dad, for taking me to places I wanted to write about and for giving me a safe and wonderful place to live.

AMANDA STANLEY. From your first comment on my blog, to enthusiastically agreeing to read my work, you have always encouraged me. Thank you for all of your prayers and for your sweet friendship! And thank you for caring for these characters since they were first introduced.

LAURA FRANTZ. You once told me that a person's writing can't help but reflect their heart. Your writing is beautiful, dear friend, and your heart even more so. Thank you for making time to uplift an aspiring author.

ELIZABETH LUDWIG. Editor and encourager extraordinaire. Thank you for beating me over the head (figuratively, of course!) with those reminders to include action beats and use less exclamation points!!! This story is much, much better-off because of your expertise and support.

RACHELLE REA. You were willing to read this story twice, and you don't know how much that means to me. Thank you for being a beta reader and my proofreader – your feedback and assistance are very much appreciated!

MICHELLE TULLER. You answered my plea for your thoughts when I was partway done with writing this story, and you responded with graciousness and enthusiasm. Now you have finally gotten to read the rest of the story – I hope you weren't disappointed!

LENA GOLDFINCH. I'm so glad I was introduced to your work via the blogosphere. Your stories and your generous friendship are inspiring. Thank you so very much for putting together such a beautiful, fitting cover, and for helping me with numerous other aspects of the finalizing process. You are one talented (and patient) person!

MY VIRGINIA CITY FRIENDS: Judy Sorensen, Karen Tassone, Desna Young, Leisa Findley (Edith Palmer's Country Inn), Gary and Nancy Teel (TNT Stagelines), and Joe Curtis (Mark Twain Bookstore). When I was doing "research" for FORGET ME NOT and BLEEDING HEART (but mostly just having the best vacations ever!), you patiently answered my questions, showed me and my family the best hospitality in the West, and made Virginia City come alive for me. Grateful for each of you!

MY TWITTER AND BLOGGER FRIENDS. You shared my joy when I revealed my cover and when I posted news about my progress. You shared my frustrations when I told you I was stressed and when I wasn't going as quickly through edits as I wished. You encouraged me in countless ways, and you helped push me through that last leg of the journey and made it an exciting time. Thank you for all you do!

Other Books in
"The Heart's Spring" Series

FORGET ME NOT
(Book 1)

When their journey leads them on unexpected paths, can two lonely hearts find the strength to remember the good amid the heartbreak?

Now available in paperback and Kindle e-book formats.

MORNING GLORY
(Book 3)

Myghal's story continues...
Summer 2014

About the Author

AMBER STOKES has a Bachelor of Science degree in English and a passion for the written word – from blogging to writing poetry, short stories, and novels. After her brief time at college in Oregon, she is now back home among the redwoods of Northern California, living life one day at a time and pursuing her passion via freelance editing and self-publishing her debut novel, BLEEDING HEART.

She loves to meet new reader and writer friends! You can connect with Amber on her blog, SEASONS OF HUMILITY, as well as on Twitter, Pinterest, and Goodreads. You can also drop her a line at amberstokes@corban.edu.

Word-of-mouth can be crucial to a new author's success.
If you enjoyed this book, please consider leaving a review online.

Thank you!